. . . .

N O
M A N ' S
L A N D

Susan Campbell Bartoletti

. . . .

No

A YOUNG

Man's

SOLDIER'S

Land

STORY

. . . .

THE BLUE SKY PRESS
An Imprint of Scholastic Inc. · New York

Special thanks to Martha Hodes, Assistant Professor
of History at New York University, for her careful check
of historical facts in the manuscript.

THE BLUE SKY PRESS

Text copyright © 1999 by Susan Campbell Bartoletti

Library of Congress catalog card number: 98-24714

ISBN 0-590-38371-X

10 9 8 7 6 5 4 3 2 1   9/9 0/0 01 02 03

Designed by Kathleen Westray

Printed in the United States of America

First printing, May 1999

. . . .

FOR MY SON,

JOE,

WITH LOVE

1

ALL THAT REMAINED of Miss Bessie was her head.

Thrasher Magee and his pap stood along the edge of the swamp. Miss Bessie's eyes were still open and surprised-looking.

Pap fingered his bushy growth of beard. "I'm right sorry to see that," he said. "She was a fine cow. Real good milker."

Fourteen-year-old Thrasher was sorry to see it, too. He liked squatting on the milking stool beside Miss Bessie, talking soft, while the cow stood sleepily, chewing cud.

Chum sniffed at the head and whined softly as Pap spat out a long stream of tobacco juice.

"Time we settle the score. Tomorrow we find where

that gator holes up, and we get him. A man don't let something take away what's his." Pap's eyes bored into Thrasher's. "If he's man enough, that is."

Pap spat again, then started back to the path that led through the piney woods to their cabin. The golden glow of his torch danced like a firefly.

Thrasher knew it wasn't his business to condemn his own father, but under his breath he cussed him anyway. "I'm man enough," he added quietly. "Just you wait and see."

EARLY THE NEXT MORNING, Pap and Thrasher poled through the swamp. Thrasher guided the punt, and his forked pole made a flat, gurgly sound each time he pushed off against the swamp bottom.

They floated past white and yellow water lilies, huckleberry high-holders, thick beds of maiden cane and purple bladderwort, and then a telltale mound of branches. An alligator nest. Thrasher and Pap eyed the bank carefully, knowing a she-gator would charge if they came too close to her eggs.

Thrasher pushed the pole harder now. A short distance farther, they reached the bank where they'd found Miss Bessie's head the night before. Pap grunted and pointed a finger. "There, boy."

Along the bank, Thrasher noted the drag marks that led to a black pool surrounded by blue-flowered pickerelweed. A gator hole. He was ready to draw that gator out and hack its spine, the only way a swamper could be sure he had himself a dead gator. Pap would be bragging on Thrasher at the Frables' next cornhusking party.

Thrasher eased over to the bank, and Pap climbed out to pull the punt ashore. Still grasping the pole, Thrasher climbed out, then made his way to the edge of the black pool. He smacked his lips loudly, the call to bring up a gator.

Nothing.

Disappointed, he jabbed the pole into the hole, once, twice. Still nothing.

"Smack on that pole," said Pap. "That gator's hard-of-hearing."

Thrasher grasped the pole tighter. He stuck the pole end between his teeth and smacked some more. His hands tingled as the sound traveled down the pole, into the murky water.

This time, the gator floated soundlessly to the surface, with barely a ripple, and its filmy lids transformed into hard, gleaming black eyes.

Pap's eyes gleamed hard and black as the gator's. With his spear, he pierced the gator's side where the tough armor turned to soft belly. The gator hissed and slapped its head. Its tail lashed. Its jaws snapped, and it bellowed.

Thrasher pulled his knife from its sheath and raised it over his head. But before the knife could fall, another roar sounded from the rushes. Out charged a female gator. The she-gator hissed, and interest flickered in Pap's eyes, a sort of amusement that now they'd have two gators to reckon with.

Thrasher gripped his knife tighter, ready to kill the gator, to hack through its spine, to be a man, but his feet wouldn't move. He stood transfixed, his feet planted as if mired in mud.

Then the she-gator rammed Pap, pushing him into the water.

THRASHER WASN'T SURE how long it had taken him to start screaming. Vaguely, he remembered Baylor Frable and his daddy gathering him up, as if he were a sack of corn. They put him in the punt and carried him back to his cabin.

The next thing he knew, evening had come. He was sitting in a chair. M'am's yellow patchwork quilt lay in folds on his lap. His sisters Mabel and Rebecca sat across from him, their faces squinched in concern. Little

Rosalie sat on Mabel's lap, and her head was cocked to one side, as if to get a closer look at him. Chum lay at his feet.

The reality of it cut deep inside Thrasher. He tried to remember one of the prayers M'am had taught him so long ago, but all he could think of was "Honor thy mother and father." The words formed a hard ball in his throat. He remembered how he had stood on the bank the night before and cussed his own father.

Somewhere outside the log cabin, a hog began to squeal, begging for its life from some unknown swamp creature. Pap's scream came to Thrasher, over and over again. He couldn't stop seeing Pap's eyes, full of disappointment.

Thrasher pressed his back against the slats of the wooden chair. The cabin air was suffocating him. He reached down to touch Chum. Chum licked his hand.

M'am put her hand on Thrasher's shoulder. At her touch, Thrasher lost all control. He didn't deserve her concern, her kindness. His tears came in great heaves.

"There, there," said M'am. She stood behind him. Her strong fingers kneaded his shoulders. "Sometimes it feels better out than in."

Thrasher gulped. He didn't feel better. He felt *weak*.

M'am stopped kneading. She stood in front of him

now. She was a tiny woman, with russet hair and a sensible face. Her belly, large with child, pushed out the front of her dress. She pressed her hand against the small of her back. He could tell her back was paining her, but she never complained.

"You ready to see your pap?" she asked.

The words rattled Thrasher. See Pap? But Pap was *dead*.

Then he remembered how it was. Womenfolk always washed the body before the burial. He tried not to think of how Pap must look.

M'am patted Thrasher's hand, urging him to his feet. "Come along. But be quiet about it. A man in his chewed-up condition needs all the rest he can get."

Chewed up? Rest? Thrasher's confusion grew.

M'am led him to the tiny lean-to bedroom and pushed the curtain aside. There, on the rush bed, lay Pap, his left leg enormous beneath a wad of bloody wrappings.

Thrasher blinked and tried to take everything in: Pap's wrapped leg. M'am's chair drawn close to the bed. A pan of red-tinged water. A needle and thread. The lines on Pap's face were smooth. He looked dead.

"Your pap's one lucky man," said M'am. "You both lucky them Frables come along when they did."

Thrasher started as he remembered—the gators,

Baylor and his daddy, a crack of rifles, the thud of knives.

Pap's eyes barely opened. "That you, boy?"

"Yes, sir."

"Been waiting on you."

Thrasher felt a rush of panic. Waiting on him? No doubt to cuss him good and tell him how soft he was.

Pap's fingers motioned to Thrasher. "Come here, boy, so I can get a look at you."

Thrasher stood at the bedside. Even in the yellow light of the grease lamp, Pap's skin looked unnaturally white.

"I'll leave y'all be," said M'am quietly. "Just for a minute. Your pap's plumb wore out."

No, Thrasher wanted to cry out. *Don't leave me.* But M'am whisked past and into the outer room.

"You look sick, boy," said Pap. His words were strained.

"Sick" didn't near describe how Thrasher felt. It was far worse than sickness. Pap reached for him, but Thrasher flinched. He couldn't bear for Pap to touch him.

Thrasher licked his lips nervously. "You remember what all happened?"

Pap winced. "No. But you must've tried to . . .

'Course you—" There was a hopeful tone, a pause in Pap's voice, as if he were waiting for Thrasher to say something. His eyes closed.

He knows, thought Thrasher, and he struggled to find words to make everything all right. But he couldn't. He was grateful to M'am, who had returned to his side. "Let Pap be now. He needs his rest."

She guided him by the elbow to the outer room and looked sorry-eyed at him. "I reckon it's hard, seeing your pap tore up like that."

Does M'am know? He forced himself to look M'am square in the eye. Her face was puffy, her eyes red-rimmed.

'Course she does, he realized. M'am always had people sense. She understood the spaces between words. No shifty peddler could cheat her on a fair price for her beeswax or Pap's pelts.

"I—I got to go," he said. The words felt fuzzy. He took his knife off the wall and slipped it into its sheath at his waist. He slung his gun over his shoulder. He had to get away. Somewhere. Anywhere.

M'am reached for him, and for a second, he thought she was going to draw him close, the way she did when he was little. But she didn't. Instead, she pulled Pap's chair out from the table. "Set a spell," she said, holding on to the back of the chair. "Baylor left some bowfin that I'm going to fry up with pork and biscuits."

Any other day, Thrasher would have jumped at M'am's cooking. But today, this morning, he couldn't bring himself to sit in Pap's chair.

"I—I'm sorry, M'am," he said. "But I can't. I—I just can't." He didn't want her reading the spaces between his words.

He slid past her and out the door, not stopping until he reached the water's edge. He knelt and cupped his hand to make a little whirlpool to draw cooler water from some deep hole—the way Pap had taught him when Thrasher was a little boy.

His stomach growled, sassing him about M'am's pork and bowfin, but he saw himself in the water, and he knew: *Ain't no place for me at Pap's table now.*

2

TRADERS HILL was a morning's walk from the Magees' cabin. As Thrasher made his way along the main street, he sensed joy in everyone around him — in the children shouldering wooden muskets and drilling in the narrow dirt streets, and in the men and women gathered on porches and street corners. How different the town was from the watery woods of the swamp.

Outside the tiny white church, Thrasher spotted Baylor's head sticking out from a knot of grammar school boys. Baylor's face lit up when he saw Thrasher, then quickly turned to concern. "How's your daddy?"

"Mending," said Thrasher with a nod. "We're mighty beholden to you and your daddy."

"Lucky we come along when we did," said Baylor. "Your pap's some man. Wrestling that gator must've been like wrestling Lucifer himself."

Panic filled Thrasher as Wade Musgrave, Jr., and his friends clamored for details. He couldn't bear to talk about it. He was grateful when Baylor turned his attention to the war.

"You come to say good-bye?" asked Baylor. "Next time you see me, I'll be sporting a gray uniform."

Thrasher was so stunned, his mouth dropped open. "You're mustering in?"

"Yessirree." Baylor nodded toward the church, then looked at Thrasher. "By the time you've grown enough peach fuzz so a company'll take you, we'll have those Yankees whupped so bad, their hindparts'll fall off."

"But you ain't eighteen," said Thrasher. "You're seventeen."

"Close enough," said Baylor.

Thrasher felt a surge of jealousy. Fourteen wasn't *near* close enough. The only way to get into the army at his age was to enlist as part of the musical corps—as a drummer boy or color bearer. "Maybe you'll see General Jackson," he said enviously.

Baylor grinned. "If I do, I'll give the general your

regards. Just you wait—the Okefinokee Rifles'll be the fightingest company ever."

THE CHURCH DOORS swung open, and Pastor Brolin stepped outside, clanging a handbell. All of Traders Hill went inside the church.

Thrasher followed Baylor. "Been quite a spell since I been in the Lord's house," he whispered to Baylor as they slid into a wooden pew near the back of the church.

"Me, too," said Baylor. "Last time we was here, Pastor jerked my daddy up for cussing chickens in the garden. We ain't been back since."

"Seems like a man ought to have the right to cuss his chickens," said Thrasher.

He looked around the sanctuary. To his right, on the long wall, two portraits gazed sternly at the congregation. One was Jefferson Davis, president of the Confederacy's provisional government. The second portrait was Alexander Stephens, vice president.

At the front, burning candles and ivy and flowers covered the long altar table. Above it hung a portrait of Jesus.

Major Flemming stood tall next to Pastor Brolin. The major rocked on his feet, waiting for the congregation to settle.

When the congregation grew quiet, the major's voice boomed. "Our Georgia needs men like you all. That's why Governor Brown has asked for another company of fine soldiers from Charlton County."

He smiled proudly. "Are you ready to be part of the mighty host that drives the enemy from our country and makes our home safe for our mothers and wives, children and sweethearts?"

The church swelled with amens and cheers. Thrasher took in all the faces of the families he knew—the Arnetts and their eight children; Wade Musgrave, Sr., his wife, and their three sons; Goodloe Watson and Miss Mary Joyce; the Garrisons; and the Tatums.

Major Flemming reached out with his hands, like Pastor Brolin at a revival meeting. "Who'll be the first to step forward?"

The church buzzed with low, urgent whispers. Thrasher watched as Goodloe Watson stepped forward; then Wade Musgrave, Sr.; then the Manning brothers; then the Robinson father and all three sons.

"Baylor," Thrasher whispered suddenly, "I'm joining."

"But you ain't old enough."

"There's got to be a way," Thrasher said.

"I reckon there is," said Baylor. "Let me think on it."

Thrasher looked around at the other families. He hoped they wouldn't give away his true age when the time came. He was pretty sure they wouldn't, because swampers held their tongues on such matters. Still, he felt nervous as he looked at the major's stern face. He wondered what the penalty was for lying to the Confederate States army.

Baylor nudged Thrasher and handed him a scrip of paper with the number *18* scratched on it. "Stick this in your shoe."

"What for?"

"That way, when the major asks how old you are, you can say 'over eighteen,' and it ain't no lie."

Thrasher did as Baylor said.

More stepped forward—the Vickery cousins, the Tatum brothers, the Hickock twins, Hazen Brown, and Baylor. Soon Thrasher, too, was standing over eighteen and feverish with excitement in the middle of an entire company.

EVERYTHING WENT QUICKLY after that. Major Flemming hurried to dispatch the men. After a thump on the chest, a few glances, a few questions, and a signature, Thrasher was sworn into the service of the Confederate States of America.

All the way home, Thrasher practiced the words he'd use to tell his family good-bye. He felt guilty, knowing how much M'am and the girls needed him right now, especially with Pap laid up and M'am in the family way.

The afternoon sun slanted low over the trees when he reached his cabin. He stood for a moment by the hollow tree, studying his home so he could carry it in his mind.

The cabins of some swampers, like the Frables and Musgraves, sorely needed repair. Their roofs sagged, and their porches were rickety and splintered. But not the Magees'. Pap made sure their pine-slash cabin sat tidy on its stilts, square in the middle of a dirt yard plucked clean of grass. The chinking filled the logs evenly, and the porch didn't squeak when a person walked across. Two rockers sat, one on each side of the butter churn. M'am's yellow curtains looked like sunshine in the two tiny windows.

Five banty hens gossiped among themselves as they scratched in the dirt near the henhouse. The hog grunted and pushed against the fencing. In the garden, Mabel and Rebecca were stooped over the rows of peas.

They'll get along fine, he told himself. *Just fine.* Mabel was thirteen and tiny like M'am but just as strong. She could swing an ax or guide the plow for Pap. At seven, Rebecca already helped with the chores. Rosalie was barely walking, but soon she'd be useful gathering eggs and picking weeds from the garden.

Chum darted across the yard and licked Thrasher's hand, then trotted alongside him over to the porch.

M'am came to the door. Rosalie toddled alongside, clutching her mother's skirt.

Rosalie reached up, and Thrasher lifted her, squeezed her, kissed the top of her head. He set her down. She plopped herself against Chum's belly, stuck her thumb in her mouth, and fingered the dog's ear.

Thrasher looked at M'am. "Next time y'all see me, I'll be sporting a gray uniform." He tried to say the words lightly, the way Baylor had earlier.

M'am reached for the rocker and gripped it. "What did you say?"

"I signed up. Me and Baylor and a heap of others from Charlton County."

"Oh, good Lord." Her face crumpled, and she sat down heavily on the rocker. She picked up her apron and cried into it, her great belly heaving.

He knelt by her and rested his head on her knees. "I got to, M'am. You can see that, can't you? I ain't never going to be man enough if I stay here. Not with Pap. Not the way he is."

She looked at him. "Can't you see? Ain't no need to conquer the world. Just conquer yourself." She picked up her apron and began to cry into it.

M'am's sobs brought the girls running from the garden. "What is it?" asked Mabel. "Is it Pap? Is it the baby?"

Thrasher stood to face his sisters. "It's me," he told them. "I joined up. With the Okefinokee Rifles. It's a crack company—"

At the news, Rebecca and Mabel looked as stunned as M'am, then they set up a wail. Rosalie's face screwed up, and she squalled, too. All the glory Thrasher had felt earlier slipped away.

M'am wiped her eyes. "You best tell Pap."

Thrasher knew he had to. He left M'am and the girls and went into the lean-to. He stood by the bed.

"Pap," he said quietly.

Pap's eyes opened to slits.

"The Twenty-sixth Georgia Regiment needs another company," said Thrasher. "And I joined up." He clenched and unclenched his hands, waiting for Pap to say something.

Nothing.

"Wait'll you see," said Thrasher. "We'll be the fightingest company ever."

Still nothing.

Pap didn't look at him. His eyes fell shut again.

Thrasher waited, waited for Pap's eyes to open, waited for Pap to have words at last to say to him, maybe even a speech about being careful not to get himself shot or killed.

But Pap didn't. Instead, his mouth formed a thin line as his jaw worked, never saying a word.

Thrasher took a deep breath, then let it out slow, grousing to himself. *I should've known better,* he thought.

He left Pap and went into the kitchen. M'am handed him two pairs of newly knitted socks and one of Pap's homespun shirts. Her mouth and chin were set firm, but her eyes betrayed her. They welled as she said, "Be careful. Choose your friends careful. And don't you start drinking whiskey or chewing tobacco or taking the Lord's name in vain."

"I won't," he promised. He took the shirt and socks and hugged them.

Mabel wrapped biscuits in a kerchief and handed him the last jar of raspberry jam, Pap's favorite. "I know what a sweet tooth you got," she whispered.

Tears trailed down Rebecca's cheeks. She gave him her cornhusk doll, then changed her mind. "I can't sleep without it," she said in a small voice as she took it back.

Rosalie just stood there, sucking her thumb and twirling her fingers around her hair. She lifted her arms and said, "Uppy uppy."

Thrasher carried her out to the porch. He hugged and kissed M'am and his sisters, then strode down the steps and across the yard. At the hollow tree, he looked back and waved.

Chum leaped from the porch and dashed across the yard to follow, but Thrasher chased him back and ordered him to stay.

Later, as Thrasher sat next to Baylor on the train that carried the Okefinokee Rifles to Camp Semmes, he thought about Chum. His heart just about broke as he thought about the hound, sitting on the porch, whining and begging with his sorrowful brown eyes.

4

IT WAS AFTER midnight. Thrasher leaned against the rail fence and wound yarn around the minie ball. He wished he had Yankees to shoot. All the Georgians wanted Yankees.

The Okefinokee Rifles had been at Camp Semmes nearly a month, but still there were no Yankees. All the fighting was taking place in Virginia, where great generals like "Stonewall" Jackson were chasing the bluecoats from the South. He continued to wind the yarn around the bullet. Here, there was little else to do with bullets except make them into baseballs.

In wartime, he thought, *you make do.*

A cool, dark breeze was moving through the trees. A few hundred yards through the woods, the rest of the

Twenty-sixth Georgia Regiment lay sleeping. Along the periphery of the camp, other Confederate pickets like himself stood duty.

"If only we had some Yankees to fight," he said.

Thrasher's own voice startled him. He hadn't meant to say the words out loud. He dropped the yarn ball and gripped his gun tighter. Wondering if anyone had heard, he peered into the darkness.

The only sound was the chirrups of crickets, the peeps and twangs of tree frogs, and the flutter of wings.

He relaxed, confident no one had heard. He groped on the ground for the yarn ball, found it, and leaned back against the fence.

As he twisted the yarn, he thought about Stonewall Jackson. He imagined the general's troops at Manassas, holding like a stone wall. *Glory,* thought Thrasher, *I wish I could've been there that day.*

Some of the soldiers poked fun at Jackson's quirks, like the way he could fall asleep anywhere or the way he always read standing up so that his organs would be properly aligned. But no one could argue that Thomas J. Jackson was the fightingest general.

Thrasher bit the yarn and knotted the end, then turned the ball, inspecting his work. It felt hard and tight. His messmates said he made the finest baseballs, and hopefully, this one would withstand Wade Musgrave's mighty swing. Satisfied, he tucked it away in his haversack.

The underbrush crackled softly. In a flash, Thrasher trained his gun into the darkness. Chances were, it wasn't a Yankee. Not this far south. Probably a possum or raccoon or turkey.

Still, you can't be too certain about Bluebellies, he told himself.

He imagined himself pointing his gun at a Yankee, taking him prisoner, and marching him back to camp. He squared his shoulders and jutted out his chin. He wished Pap could see him now, in his gray uniform.

He held the pleasant thought in his mind until it wavered and disappeared, just like every other pleasant idea when it met up with thoughts of Pap.

More stirring came out of the underbrush, then a soft warble.

Turkey. Disappointed, he relaxed and lowered his gun. The warble came again. *Turkey'd taste mighty fine for tomorrow's dinner.* He warbled in response, then listened for another call.

He fingered the trigger, knowing full well he couldn't shoot. Not now. Not on picket duty. One shot from him and the entire sleeping regiment would spring to life, dressed and ready to fight the enemy.

The underbrush crackled again, much too loudly this time for a turkey. Excited, Thrasher tightened his grip on the gun. He hoped he could keep his voice from cracking. "Halt!" he called out. "Who goes there?"

"Just us turkeys," came the response.

"That's right," said another. "Just us turkeys."

Thrasher recognized the voices of his messmates Baylor Frable and Tim LaFaye, having fun at his expense. "Show yourselves," he said, "or I'm going to shoot now and ask questions later!"

The two boys stepped out of the shadows. Even in the darkness, there was no mistaking Baylor's long, skinny frame, hooked beak of a nose, and monstrous Adam's apple. Tim was shorter, eye-level with Thrasher, but thin and less gawky than Baylor. He had dark hair and deep, dark eyes that showed little white. When he moved, he reminded Thrasher of a fine colt.

Thrasher lowered his gun. "You boys are lucky y'all don't get yourselves plucked making calls like that."

"Don't be sore," said Baylor. He took a biscuit from his haversack and handed it to Thrasher. "We conscripted these from a widow beyond the hill. She said Tim reminded her of her youngest boy."

"She even invited us back for dinner," said Tim.

"Her daughters was sweet on us," said Baylor. "You

should've seen them, Thrasher. Twittering like a couple of blue jays."

Thrasher bit into the biscuit and chewed slowly. *Mmm.* It was prime, nearly as flaky as M'am's. "Ain't you boys supposed to be on picket duty?"

Baylor gulped his biscuit down. "Yeah, but we was hungry. Besides, ain't like there's Yankees around. Coastal defense is as exciting as guarding a honey pot from flies."

Thrasher knew Baylor didn't give a hog's tail about Yankees. Baylor wanted adventure, and war promised lots of that.

Still, he thought, *it wouldn't hurt Baylor to take soldiering more seriously.* Baylor could barely snap off a salute, even though they spent countless hours drilling and practicing maneuvers. But it was pointless to argue with him. Thrasher reached for another biscuit instead.

Baylor unbuttoned his coat and stretched out on the grass. Pickets weren't allowed to sit or let their guns touch the ground, another regulation that didn't bother Baylor.

Tim remained standing next to Thrasher. "Some days I wonder if we'll ever find Yankees to fight," he said, smothering a yawn with his hand. "What do you suppose it'll be like?"

Thrasher was surprised. He wondered if Tim ever lay

awake at night the way Thrasher did, praying that when the time came to fight, he wouldn't run.

Thrasher doubted it. The others all regarded Tim as some sort of hero. At sixteen, Tim was too young to fight, yet he wanted to fight so bad that he had escaped New Orleans in March, after martial law had been declared. He made his way to Traders Hill, where he knew nary a soul, and mustered into the Okefinokee Rifles. Soon after they arrived at Camp Semmes, they heard that New Orleans had fallen to the Yankees.

"I suppose," Baylor said slowly, "that fighting a Yankee's the same as meeting up with a bad-humored bear. You stand up to him. Did I ever tell you about the time I fought off a bear with nothing but a honey pot?"

"A heap of times," said Thrasher. "But you disremember that your daddy buried an ax in that bear's head. That's why the bear was in a foul mood."

Tim chuckled. "I should have known."

Thrasher laughed, too. For a moment, it felt like home. On Saturday nights, Baylor often stopped by their cabin and sat on their porch, telling jokes and tall tales, and getting M'am and the girls a-giggling. Mable, Rebecca, and even little Rosalie were sweet on Baylor.

Suddenly, somewhere along the picket line, a rifle cracked. A single shot. There was a pause, then a second shot.

Thrasher's heart fluttered and turned over.

Baylor leaped to his feet. "Yankees!"

"Hold on," said Thrasher, getting up. "We got to wait on orders."

"Orders! Who cares about orders!" Baylor's unbuttoned coat flapped about him like the huge wings of a horned owl as he took off toward camp through the woods.

Thrasher stamped the ground, counting the seconds. He fingered the leather shot bag that hung from his belt. It held twenty paper cartridges of gunpowder and minie balls. Tim held his gun tightly and stared in the direction of camp.

At last, a bugle flared, calling all pickets back to camp. Tim let out a Rebel yell, then took to his heels through the woods. His cartridge belt clinked in the night as he ran.

Thrasher knew he had to follow, but he couldn't. He stood there like a frightened marsh rabbit. It was just like back at home, standing with Pap at the edge of the gator hole. His feet were mired in mud.

CHAPTER

5

SHAME CUT THROUGH Thrasher like a knife. At last, he willed his feet to move and stumbled through the woods back to camp.

He heard excited voices before he even reached the outskirts of the camp.

When he broke out of the woods, the camp looked like a field of fireflies. Men milled about, holding blazing torches, their faces glowing eerily. They were in various stages of dress—pants on, pants off, shoes on, shoes off, some holding guns.

Thrasher felt confused. *Where's the lines*, he wondered, *the guns, the snare drums?*

He pushed through the knots of men until he spotted Wade Musgrave's balding head.

"Why ain't we in formation?" asked Thrasher.

Wade chuckled. "Warn't Yankees, son. Just cows." He tipped his head in the direction where Hazen Brown and Major Wilmot stood.

Hazen Brown reminded Thrasher of a fat toad, moody and prim. He'd been friendly enough when they arrived at camp, when he'd hoped to be elected an officer. But he wasn't elected, and he remained a common foot soldier like the rest of them.

"I heard a jingling," Hazen was saying to the major. He gestured emphatically, and his voice squeaked. "It could've been Yankees, disguised with cowbells."

Baylor emerged from another group. He was carrying a steaming cup in his hands. "Y'all hear?" he asked. "Hazen can't even hit the broad side of a cow." He held out the cup, offering a sip to Thrasher.

Thrasher took the cup and sipped the bitter liquid. They had run out of coffee days ago and had to settle for a watery amber brew made from sweet potatoes.

He looked back at Hazen. "Damn dark," Hazen was saying. "I couldn't see a thing." Even though Thrasher didn't care much for Hazen, he felt sorry for him, standing there, shamefaced.

Major Wilmot was rubbing his shoulder as he listened to Hazen's excuses. Thrasher wondered if Wilmot's shoulder was still paining him from the fall he had taken a few days ago from his horse. Thrasher liked

Wilmot. A smooth-shaven, middle-aged man, he was tough but fair. Never asked his men to do anything he wouldn't expect of himself.

"Did you call out?" asked the major.

"Yes, sir," said Hazen.

"Order them to show themselves?"

"Yes, sir."

"Ask for the password?"

"Yes, sir."

"When they didn't comply, you fired?"

"They didn't give the password, sir."

A group of men guffawed. Wilmot silenced them with a stern look. "Then you are to be commended for following orders," said Wilmot. "No harm done, aside from rousing your fellow soldiers from their sleep."

Thrasher could see the relief wash over Hazen. Hazen straightened his shoulders and snapped off a salute. Wilmot dismissed him with a nod.

THE NEXT AFTERNOON, Thrasher sat on a log. In front of him, an overturned cracker crate served as a table. He stared at the blank sheet of paper. He had paid the camp sutler a whole dollar for a quire of paper, a short stack of envelopes, and a pencil.

The pencil felt awkward in Thrasher's hand, not natural like a gun or fishing pole. The words felt awkward, too.

Time and time again he had tried to choose the words that would tell Pap that he was doing something important. Each time he tried to set the words down, they slipped away from him.

For some people, words were easy. Like Goodloe Watson, who was studying to be a preacher. Or Baylor, who always told the funniest stories, even if they weren't all true. Or even Tim, who wrote letters for the soldiers who couldn't. Tim's handwriting crept like vines across the page.

Disgusted, Thrasher folded the paper, slipped it into his haversack, and put the pencil away. He took out the yarn baseball. Maybe Baylor would want to practice catching.

In the clearing past the rows of white canvas dog tents, a company was drilling. They couldn't get left-face, right-face, about-face together yet. His own feet still felt sore from the extra drills his company did that morning, thanks to Baylor for saying a woodpecker had more drum in him than the drummer.

At the other end of the field, a group of Wiregrass Minutemen were playing baseball. Cheers went up as the ball lobbed between the second and third basemen. The Wiregrass Minutemen were good—really good. Thrasher and the rest of the Okefinokee Rifles couldn't wait to lame them in a game real soon.

He turned and squinted toward the officers' quarters. Some of the officers had brought slaves from home, and Thrasher saw a Negro tending kettles over a fire. Two others were washing clothes, and another was splitting wood. Beyond them, he spotted Baylor and Tim.

Thrasher took off his cap and waved. "Want to play catch?" he called.

"Can't," Baylor hollered. "Looky here," he said as he got closer. He was carrying a canning jar and a tin dinner plate. Baylor held up the jar to show off the lice crawling around inside.

The sight made Thrasher itch all over. Lice—or graybacks, the men called them—showed no regard for rank. They infested everyone, from officer to private. "What are you doing with them graybacks?" he asked.

Baylor grinned, showing off the gap between his front teeth. M'am claimed the gap meant a generous nature. She was right. Baylor shared most everything, whether it belonged to him or not.

"I been learning them all morning. And now they're so smart, I reckon they're kin to General Stonewall Jackson's very own graybacks."

Thrasher shook his head in amazement. "You can't read nor write yourself. The only thing you're good at is figuring."

"And right now I figure to make myself some money."

Thrasher tucked the baseball away. He followed Baylor and Tim over to several Twiggs County privates who were smoking and playing cards outside their tents. A cloud of tobacco smoke hung in the air.

Baylor held the jar up. "Get your money up and choose your grayback," he called out. "And if these graybacks don't suit you, there's plenty more where they come from." He scratched beneath his shirt.

"I got a whole battalion of the critters," said a boy who appeared to be Baylor's age. His long nose and skinny neck reminded Thrasher of an egret. "They all sing me to sleep at night."

"That ain't nothing," said Baylor. "My graybacks and me are such good friends that if I was to lay down right here, they'd carry me to Vir-ginny."

They laughed the way they always did at Baylor's jokes. Eagerly, they gathered around Baylor as he unscrewed the lid of the jar and shook the lice onto the plate. With his finger, he pushed them to the edge while Tim passed his cap around. Five men dropped coins into the cap and selected a grayback.

"Ready, set, crawl," said Baylor. He flicked the plate with a snap of his finger. The graybacks crawled back and forth.

"Go, go, go!" they shouted as if they were watching a horse race.

Five of the graybacks scurried in circles, but Baylor's grayback struck a beeline for the opposite edge of the plate. He scuttled first across the finish line.

The skinny egret boy jumped up, letting loose a string of curses. "Damn vermin!" he shouted. "I can't take them anymore!"

He kicked off his shoes and dropped his pants and woolen drawers. Naked, he picked up a cookpot and covered his privates. "Anyone else going to boil their clothes?" he asked, looking around.

The others pulled off their shirts and stripped down to baggy woolen drawers or even less.

"You joining us?" a burly man asked Baylor. "It's the only way to parole them graybacks."

Baylor scratched at his stomach. "Naw. I couldn't sleep without a few gnawing at me."

The man turned to Tim. "How about you? Or are you too shy to let us see you was hit by the same windstorm that blew the hairs off this feller's chest?" He jabbed his thumb at Thrasher.

"No fair," protested Thrasher. He yanked his shirt over his head and stuck out his chest. "I sprouted three or four hairs since last week."

He was amused to see Tim's face had turned bright pink. "Glory, Tim," he said pointedly. "Ain't nothing to be shy about. Don't you rich fellers ever swim in New Orleans?"

Another man handed a cookpot to Tim. "You can cover your lonely soldier and haversacks with this."

Tim's eyes narrowed. He pushed the pot away. "Let's get our guns, Baylor," he said. "I feel like shooting something."

Thrasher waited, hoping they'd invite him, but they didn't. He watched Baylor and Tim lope past and into the tall grass, carrying their guns and empty sacks.

Annoyed, he kicked at a red clod of dirt. It was unfair. Why didn't Tim join some Louisiana regiment? That's where he belonged—with the fancy Zouaves, who sported red baggy trousers and matching felt hats—not with the Okefinokee Rifles.

"Hey, boy," the burly man called to Thrasher. "You coming?"

"Boy," muttered Thrasher. Even in war, some things felt the same as home.

With a sigh, he picked up the last cookpot and followed the others down the stony path leading to the river. Other Rebels were already there, boiling their clothes and swimming as contented as otters in a river dotted with paper sailboats.

6

THAT EVENING, Thrasher joined his mess-
mates by the fire. Baylor, Tim, and Wade sat on a blanket, slapping at bugs as they played poker.

Thrasher wished they had invited him to play. But
they hadn't, and he was too stubborn to invite himself
the way Wade had.

He thought of the Sunday a few years back, when
Baylor had taught him to play. They had sat on the
porch, playing for peanuts. M'am had been fitified
when she caught them playing cards on the Lord's day,
and she had shooed Baylor home.

A mosquito drilled into Thrasher's ankle. He slapped
at it, flicked it away, and looked back at the poker game.

"Baylor, your fondness for gambling ranks second
only to your fondness for stealing," said Wade.

"Ain't stealing in the army," said Baylor. "It's foraging."

They all laughed. So far, Baylor's foraging exploits had yielded chickens, a smoked ham, a hog that gave them all a lively chase through camp, boiled puddings, condensed milk, and once, even chocolates. Thanks to Baylor, their meals were often the envy of the camp, although never as tasty as M'am's.

"Hey, Preacher," Baylor called to Goodloe. "Does the Bible got any commandments against foraging?"

Goodloe looked up from the tattered New Brunswick newspaper he was reading. His glasses reflected the firelight. "No, I suppose not," he said. He folded the newspaper and set it down. "War changes most everything, doesn't it?"

Hazen sipped his coffee loudly. Even from where Thrasher sat, he could smell it. They all longed for some, but were too proud to ask Hazen, who received weekly stashes of food and clothing from home. His sister Cordelia even sent a feather pillow she had stuffed herself.

"I wish fighting orders would come down soon," said Hazen. "I'm fixing to part those Bluebellies like wheat before the scythe. Like Moses before the Red Sea. Like Jackson at Manassas—"

Baylor looked up from his cards. "Like the way you parted them cows."

Wade cupped his hands around his mouth. "Moo-oo-o."

Hazen scowled. "I followed orders. Even the major said so—"

Nobody listened to Hazen's protests. It was Wade's turn to bet. He dropped several cards in the middle of the blanket, then took out his whiskey flask. He gave it a shake. Empty. "Wish I had some whiskey," he said. "A good drink's always fitting with a game of cards."

"You know whiskey ain't allowed in camp," said Baylor, in mock seriousness.

"If there's a camp rule," said Wade, "it's you, Baylor, who'll figure out a way to break it." He made a grand display of dropping two dollars in the middle of the blanket.

Two whole dollars! Thrasher was surprised at Wade. Two dollars could buy a heap of things for Wade's boys.

"Wade must reckon he's got a pretty good hand," said Baylor to Tim. "But it can't be too good, or we'd see the sweat pop out on that bald head of his."

Wade growled and mopped his head with his sleeve.

Thrasher watched as Tim tentatively added two wrinkled Confederate bills to the small pile of money in the center of the blanket.

Tim's a peculiar feller, thought Thrasher. He supposed it had to do with Tim being from New Orleans. In some ways, Tim was just like the rest of them. He liked to hunt and fish and joke around. And like Goodloe, he liked to read and talk about poetry.

But if you teased Tim about his uppity ways—like the way he wouldn't use the latrine with the others—he'd get as riled up as a rattlesnake. He'd stomp off from camp with his gun, just as he had done earlier that day. He always came back in better humor and with a dead sack of possum, rabbit, or squirrel.

Thrasher had felt awkward in the beginning, too, when he measured himself against the others. Nobody was fourteen like him, though plenty of boys the same age as Baylor and Tim had signed up. Most men, it seemed, were in their twenties, like Goodloe and Hazen. Some appeared to be Wade's age, and some were even as old as Pap.

But Thrasher was over his awkwardness now, and when he saw soldiers who preferred to creep off into the woods to take care of their needs, it seemed silly. Did they think they had something nobody else did?

Wade discarded a card and drew a new one. With a sigh, Tim turned in two cards. "Don't sigh," said Baylor. "You're giving yourself away."

Baylor threw away three cards and picked new ones. His face was expressionless, his mouth a straight line, the glitter gone from his eyes. It was impossible to read Baylor, even for Thrasher. But

Wade pulled out three dollars. *Don't,* Thrasher wanted to warn him. Put it away. Quit now. Send it home. But

Wade was headstrong. He wouldn't throw off once he had made up his mind. He was as persistent as Chum on the scent trail of a raccoon.

Tim matched Wade's bet, but Baylor raised it a dollar. Wade's temper fired up. "You're bluffing," he said to Baylor. "I know you are."

"So call it, then," said Baylor.

"I will." Wade dug in his pants pocket for another dollar and tossed it down. "That's it. All I've got."

Tim hesitated a moment, then lay down a dollar. Thrasher cringed. *Baylor's gonna wipe you out,* he thought.

Baylor placed his cards down—a six, seven, eight, nine, and ten of spades.

Wade threw down his hand—a pair of aces and a pair of kings.

"That's a good hand," said Baylor. "Real good. But not good enough to beat my straight flush."

"Why, you confounded—" blustered Wade.

Baylor swept the money toward himself. "Pleasure doing business with y'all."

Tim stopped Baylor. "I have one of those straights, too." Speechless, Baylor gaped as Tim spread his cards on the blanket—the nine, ten, jack, queen, and king of diamonds.

Tim counted out the dollar bills and coins, then gave a satisfied smile as he tucked the money into his pants pocket. "Perhaps when the war's over, I'll make my home in Georgia. I like the way you boys play."

Goodloe whacked at a mosquito on his arm and inched closer to the fire. "No place better than Georgia," he said. "After the fever took my family, I lived with my momma's Yankee cousins in Pennsylvania. They reared me like I was one of their own, and I stayed so long, I lost my drawl. But it was waiting for me when I moved back home."

Home. Thrasher closed his eyes for a moment, and he was back home, done with his evening chores, sitting on the splintery cabin porch with Chum.

Chum was a fine dog, no under-the-porch-sleeper like some. Over the years, Thrasher had taught Chum everything a good hound ought to know, from flushing out turkeys to leaping out of a boat to retrieve an otter without leaving a toothmark.

Suddenly, Thrasher was filled with a longing to scratch between Chum's ears, torn and scarred from a scrap with a bad-humored black bear that had been after one of their eating hogs last winter.

Immediately, he became sore with himself. He hated the feeling of being homesick.

Besides, Thrasher reminded himself, at the mustering in, didn't Major Flemming himself promise that the war wouldn't last more than a few months? We'd be home to harvest our crops and butcher our fall hogs.

I hope Chum remembers me by then, he thought.

THRASHER POURED himself some sweet potato coffee, then reached into his pocket for a leftover johnnycake. He broke it in two and offered a piece to Goodloe. He felt comfortable next to Goodloe. There was something calming about him. Goodloe was never in a hurry and always explained things in a patient way. He never looked through a person the way Hazen did, and he never hollered or criticized like Pap.

"I can't imagine living up North," said Thrasher.

Goodloe dunked the cake into his tin cup. "Don't get me wrong," he said. He inspected the coffee's surface for the maggots that usually crawled out of the cake. "I love my cousins, even if they are Bluebellies. But Yankees don't understand us and our ways. They can't see it's the land we're fighting for, and the right to speak the way we do and live the way we do."

"Amen," said Hazen. He raised his cup to Goodloe in salute. "The South has been without equal representation in Congress for years. The North imposes tariffs, then uses the money to build themselves railroads, factories, and mills. Meantime, the South gets nothing.

The North doesn't have the right to force their ways on us."

"Nobody's got the right to force their ways on nobody else," said Thrasher. He thought of Pap. There was only one way to clean the barn, chink the logs, set a trap. Pap's way.

No matter how hard Thrasher tried, he couldn't please Pap, who always found something to criticize—a chore not done fast enough or soon enough or well enough to suit him. "A man's character shows in his respect for his work," he always said in a scolding voice. "Respect your work, no matter what kind of work it is. Respect the sweeping, respect the mending, respect the plowing."

It was easier for Thrasher's sisters. Mabel pleased Pap by making a batch of apple-butter muffins or a sweet potato pie. Rebecca could bring a smile to Pap by dancing while he played his fiddle. Rosalie pleased Pap by lifting her arms and saying, "Uppy uppy." Pap would swing her up onto his shoulders.

Once Thrasher had asked M'am, "Why ain't nothing I do ever good enough for Pap?"

The pain M'am had felt for Thrasher had lined her face, but she hadn't let on. "Pap don't like weakness any more than fear," she'd said. "That's the way some men are. Strength comes from overing your fear."

Weakness. Fear. He hated the thought of it.

He had felt afraid when Pap had first given him the long rifle, and he'd sighted his first deer. He hadn't been sure he was strong enough to kill something so big and so beautiful. But he had fired the gun because Pap was standing there, right behind him, waiting.

He had felt afraid again when Pap had made him stick his first hog. He'd plunged the curved knife into the hog's throat, feeling its skin rip as he'd pulled the knife across the hog's neck, because Pap was right behind him, watching that, too.

The trick, he'd known, was to remove himself from what he was doing, as if someone else's hand were holding the knife. He'd shallowed his breathing until he was floating somewhere above the squealing hog and the bloody knife. He'd blocked out the sight, the sound, and the smell, but he had never overed his fear.

Thrasher looked at his messmates, their faces shadowed in the firelight, and he wondered if they ever felt afraid and shamed by it. He wished he could ask Goodloe or Wade, but he knew better.

Goodloe pushed his glasses against the bridge of his nose, and his voice grew earnest and beseeching. "Still, as different as my Yankee cousins and I are, I pray I won't face them in battle."

Thrasher looked into the fire. *Sometimes you fight the people you grow up with even without war,* he thought.

7

THRASHER WAS GRATEFUL when the last bugle sounded. Goodloe doused the dying fire with the remainder of his sweet potato coffee, and Thrasher crawled into the canvas tent he shared with Baylor and Tim. He rolled up a sour-smelling shirt and tucked it beneath his head like a pillow.

He no longer heard Baylor and Tim talking outside. He wondered where they took off to. Not that it mattered much. He didn't need them. Besides, three in a tent didn't leave much elbow room, and he was tired of being stuck in the middle. Baylor and Tim both insisted on sleeping on the outside.

Thrasher dreamed he was home, standing at the edge of the swamp as Chum lapped at the water.

Nearby, a floating log lazily rolled against a bed of water lilies.

Suddenly, the log transformed into a mossy bull gator that burst out of the water. It lunged and grabbed hold of the dog. Thrasher knew what he needed to do: He had to take his knife and hack the gator's spine. *This gator ain't taking what's mine.*

But Thrasher couldn't move. He stood there, his feet planted in mud. He watched in horror as the gator dragged Chum underwater.

He awoke to find himself reaching for the loose skin of Chum's neck, to comfort himself. His fingers found the empty blankets left by Baylor and Tim.

Outside, he heard a stirring and the whisper of voices. The tent flapped open, and Thrasher was grateful to see Baylor and Tim. Baylor was stooped beneath the weight of a huge watermelon.

"Baylor!" said Thrasher. "You been stealing melons?"

Hic! "No." Whiskey oozed from Baylor's breath. "A farmer's daughter give me this melon. You should've seen her. Tiniest waist this side of Georgia." He sighed. "I promised to name my musket after her."

Baylor set the melon down on Thrasher's blanket, then slipped his gun from over his shoulder and planted a kiss on the barrel. "My dear Miss Laura Lee."

Tim edged his way into the tent and slumped down next to Thrasher. He reeked of whiskey and tobacco. "Baylor," said Tim. "There's more to girls than tiny waists."

Baylor clapped Tim on the back. "You're right. There's ankles and feet and"—he stooped to suck on a reed poking out of the melon's middle—"Mm-mm." He wiped his mouth with his hand. "Thrasher, as our tent mate, you can help yourself to two dips of your goozling for free. Everybody else I'm charging two bits."

"Two bits! For melon?"

"This ain't no ordinary melon," said Baylor. "Try it."

Thrasher sucked on the reed. His mouth was warmed by a heavy, sweet taste. "Whiskey?" He pulled back and whistled.

"No need to thank me," said Baylor. "I hollowed out her middle and filled her up." He lowered his voice and confessed, "The whiskey's the part I stole when Miss Laura Lee's daddy wasn't looking."

NEWS OF THE WATERMELON whiskey traveled quickly. Within five minutes, a straggly group waited outside Thrasher's tent, hoping for a swallow. Barefooted and clad in baggy woolen drawers, they joked as they dropped coins in Baylor's cap.

"Baylor," said the skinny-necked boy from Twiggs

County, "you could swipe the buttons off an officer's coat during inspection."

Hazen came by, but unlike the others, he wore a white cotton nightshirt and carpet slippers. "Baylor never takes anything seriously," he complained. "I doubt if he'll ever do his duty."

Thrasher clenched his fist. He felt like giving Hazen a shot in the holler. How dare he say such a thing about Baylor—even if it was true.

But before Thrasher could pop him, Hazen suddenly snapped to attention. "Major!" he exclaimed with a salute.

Major Wilmot nodded briefly and strode briskly toward Baylor. Everyone stepped out of his way.

Someone nudged Baylor, who was in the middle of a story Thrasher had heard before—about an outsider who was treed by wild rooters for three days in the swamp.

Thrasher braced himself. But to his surprise, Major Wilmot dropped two coins into Baylor's hat. "I hear two bits is enough to wet my whistle."

The men and boys grinned and elbowed each other as the major stopped and took his turn at the melon. He wiped his mouth on his hand and climbed atop a tree stump.

They all fell quiet. Thrasher knew Wilmot must have something powerfully important to say.

"I was saving this news for morning inspection," said Wilmot. "But perhaps it's better to hear it with whiskey."

Thrasher held his breath.

Wilmot hooked his thumbs through his suspenders. "We've got orders to cook three days' rations." He looked around the circle of boys and men. "Jackson needs us Georgians to help him drive the Yankees from Virginia."

"Ya-hoo!" hollered Baylor. He and Tim looped arms and spun around in a circle.

Hats sailed in the air. Several men linked arms and danced. A mouth harp trilled "Dixie," and another encored with "Bonny Blue Flag."

"Jackson," said Thrasher, rolling the name over in his mouth. "Now ain't that something?"

8

THRASHER WAS UP LONG before reveille the next morning. He pulled his blanket out from under Baylor and crawled outside.

He stood, stretched, and scratched at his stomach. He had slept well, he realized. Strangely well. No nightmares. No monsters. He felt good, more rested than he had felt in a long time.

He spread his blanket on the ground and smoothed out the wrinkles and rolled it tightly. *What incredible luck for the Georgians to be placed with General Jackson,* he thought as he rolled the blanket. Incredible luck, indeed.

After packing his haversack, he made himself eggs and biscuits in a black pan over the fire. His stomach felt warm and full.

Thrasher liked the early part of morning best, when he could sit and watch the rest of the army awaken around him. Hazen, Wade, and Goodloe emerged, one at a time, from their tent.

Goodloe washed up first, splashing water on his face. He washed and dried his glasses. Hazen took more time washing up, carefully trimming and waxing his mustache until the ends were curled like mice tails. Wade didn't wash at all but spent a good deal of time scratching.

Baylor lifted the tent flap. He stood, blinking and swaying slightly in the morning sun. Behind him, Tim stretched like a sleepy cat. Overhead, birds chattered loudly.

Slowly, the camp came to life, and the smell of pork and eggs cooking filled the air. Everywhere men were preparing rations, eating, washing up, rolling blankets and tents, and packing haversacks.

At last the bugle flared orders. The Twenty-sixth Georgia boarded the train that would carry them to Virginia.

Those Yankees'll see, Thrasher thought as he climbed into the waiting boxcar. *Nobody's got the right to force their ways on anybody else. Not the Yankees. Not Abraham Lincoln. Not Pap.*

An image of Pap and the gator flashed before him,

but he pushed it down. *I'll fight,* he told himself. *Just you wait and see.*

THE TRAIN WAS CROWDED and hot. So crowded, they slept sitting up. So murderously hot, seven men died from heat alone. So suffocating that Thrasher and others, desperate for air, knocked airholes in the boxcars with their rifle butts. Some rode with their heads stuck out the airholes. Others, like Baylor, clung like bees to the outside of the cars.

After several days of insufferable heat, the train poked its way into the outskirts of Richmond. Thrasher vied with the others for a peek of the city through the airholes.

"Glory!" said Thrasher. "Looky them piles and piles of dirt!" He moved so Goodloe could stick his head through the airhole.

"Earthworks," said Goodloe. "They're dug for protection around the city. To keep the Federals out."

Thrasher whistled. Federals. It was hard to believe they were so close.

At last, the train pulled into the Richmond station. As the Georgians descended the steps, a band played "Dixie." Swarms of men, women, and children had turned out to greet the regiment.

Thrasher took a deep breath. Fresh Virginia air. How good it felt. How good it smelled.

Everywhere he turned, old men were patting him and shaking his hand. Women and their daughters smiled at him and hugged him. Trays of food—sweet-smelling cakes, meats, and cheese—were passed around by girls who reminded him of his sisters. He tipped his hat and thanked them as he ate and drank and filled his pockets.

"God bless you," said a white-haired man in a deco-rated uniform. "You're a fine-looking soldier. I was your age when I headed out for the War of 1812. Fought again in the Mexican War. Helped us win California. Now men like you are helping the South."

Men like you. Thrasher basked in the compliment and shook the man's hand vigorously. Thrasher *was* a man—just like Goodloe and Wade and the others. *If only Pap could see me now.*

THE SUN WAS BROILING. Thrasher's wool uniform was soaked with sweat, which made him in-credibly itchy. He took his hat off and mopped his fore-head with his sleeve. He wished he could escape behind a building or into a carriage lane where he could give himself a good private scratching.

He squeezed through the crowd and found Baylor

and Tim near the end of the train platform. Baylor tipped his hat to two girls, and both of them pressed slips of paper into Baylor's hands before fluttering away.

Thrasher could see that Tim was jealous over Baylor's popularity, and it amused him. The streets were brimming with pretty girls. No sense fussing over a few who were taken in by Baylor's gap-toothed smile and sunburned face.

Baylor circled an arm around yet another girl's waist and snatched a cake from the tray she was carrying. "Didn't nobody never tell you what a perfect wayside lily you are?" he asked.

The girl slipped from Baylor's arm. Her skirts switched like an angry cat's tail. "Yes," she said. "My husband."

Baylor laughed. He saluted her and blew her a kiss as she whisked away, then he stuffed the cake into his mouth. "Ain't war grand?" he said, happy-eyed. He handed the slips of paper to Tim. "What do these say?"

"You know your figures," said Tim briskly. "Isn't it time you learned your letters?" He unfolded the papers. "This one has the name and address of a Miss Marybelle Swisher and the other of a Miss Jolene Buchanan."

"I'm in clover! Now I got two more names for my gun."

"You only got one gun, Baylor," said Thrasher.

"Not for long. I hear there's good pickings after a fight." Baylor took the papers back from Tim and pressed them to his chest, letting out an exaggerated sigh. "Mm-mm. Vir-ginny girls smell like roses and lilacs. Nothing like the girls back home."

He grinned at Thrasher. "Wait and see, time's a-coming. You'll care what girls smell like, too."

Thrasher scowled. He sniffed his jacket and made another face. It had been more than a week since he had washed or changed his clothes. "I bet you them girls ain't thinking how swell any of us smell."

Baylor wasn't listening. A red-haired girl in a light green dress passed by. He rubbed his hands together and gazed longingly after her. "I'll see you fellers later."

"Fool," muttered Tim.

"Come on," said Thrasher. "Let's find something better to do."

CHAPTER

9

THRASHER AND TIM passed some of the army buildings—the commissary, the signal corps, the mail service, the provost marshal—and passed uniformed men of all ranks hurrying along the streets.

"Feels good to walk without worrying about left-right-left," said Thrasher, and Tim agreed.

They counted four hospitals, all looking newly erected. Everywhere male nurses bustled, carrying baskets of cloth and other medical supplies and food.

The cobbled streets were jammed with carriages and delivery wagons and ambulances. The sidewalks were crowded with people, black and white, all hastening to get someplace else.

Thrasher whistled in amazement. "Richmond ain't nothing like Traders Hill."

"Richmond isn't like New Orleans either," said Tim. "In New Orleans the buildings are all different colors—yellow, sea green, soft pink, and even chocolate. They're trimmed with iron balconies, some two or three stories high, no two patterns alike. And there are restaurants and theater and opera."

He looked at Thrasher. "After this war is over, you should visit New Orleans. I'll introduce you to Mama and Papa—and you'll meet Chaucer, too."

"Chaucer?"

"My parrot. He greets everyone with *'Buenos días! Adieu! Allez-vous en!'* He is a stupid bird; he can't keep his French and Spanish straight."

"A talking bird? You're pulling my leg!" Thrasher laughed out loud at the thought.

He looked back at Tim again and saw that Tim's lips had hardened into a bitter frown. "Who knows what the Yankees have done to my home," said Tim.

"What was it like, having Yankees so close?"

"Before I left, we had taken up the carpets and packed up the house. We buried the silver, and Mama sewed all her jewelry into the hems of her dresses. Nearly every woman carried a seven-shooter and knew how to use it. And now—" Tim stopped. "I'm sorry. I just can't talk about it."

Thrasher couldn't imagine the anger he'd feel if Yankees ever took over the Okefinokee.

They walked in silence past more buildings and stores, past narrow cobbled streets overcrowded with horses and buggies. "Tell me about the Okefinokee," Tim said.

Thrasher sighed. "I can't tell it the way you do. You talk pretty as Goodloe."

"Just tell it your own way."

"I can't. I can't even start."

"Start in the morning. What's the swamp like in the morning?"

The morning. "That's the best time for poling," said Thrasher. He spoke hesitantly, trying to collect his thoughts. "Early, when the water's high, after the summer rains have come."

"Poling?"

"I use a long, forked pole to guide my punt. Chum—that's my dog—sits in the bow."

"What does Chum do?"

"His nose sniffs this way and that. He's all a-quiver to jump out and fetch a marsh rabbit, if I'll oblige him by shooting one."

"And you?"

"I prod my way through the neverwets and water lilies."

For a second, Thrasher saw Pap. Pap's hands were outstretched, reaching for him, needing him.

Ought he tell Tim about the gators? Thrasher swallowed hard, blinked, shook his head. He chased Pap away.

"Farther up," he continued, "a bull gator's napping on a log throne. He's so big, his eyes are sixteen inches from his nostrils. Know what that means?"

"Tell me."

"That gator's at least that many feet long. Sixteen."

"Sixteen feet!"

"Soon the sun's poking over the treetops. And somewhere, you hear the sweetest lullabies being sung."

"Lullabies? Who's singing?"

"The black snake. She's the wife of the diamondback rattler, and she sings so sweet that outsiders come looking for her. But look out. Once they find her, her jealous husband bites their hands. Outsiders ain't never seen again."

"You're pulling my leg. A snake can't sing."

"Your parrot can talk French and Spanish?"

"Yes, but—"

"Then a black snake can sing," said Thrasher. "Ask Baylor. There's plenty of outsiders who never come out the swamp. But if a feller can read the bark growth and knows the osprey nests, he won't never find himself lost."

"You ever get lost?" asked Tim.

"Never," said Thrasher. Tim didn't need to know about all the times he was misplaced.

"When this war is over," said Tim, "I'd be grateful if you'd take me poling."

"That would suit me fine," said Thrasher.

The boys trudged along in silence. Talking about the swamp made Thrasher terribly homesick. The more brick and glass and tall columns he saw, the more he longed for thick-bearded cypresses, a punt boat, and Chum.

SOON THE BOYS STOPPED outside a general merchandise store. They looked through the doorway, and Thrasher spotted glass jars of black licorice, honey taffy, and stick candy. His mouth watered.

He headed for the counter, bought a piece of stick candy, and popped it in his mouth.

Maybe Mabel, Rebecca, and Rosalie would like pretty ribbons for their hair. He looked around the store. Tim was picking out thread and buttons.

Behind Tim, he saw fancy hats and carved smoking pipes. On the far wall, knives were displayed—

pearl-handled knives like Tim's, jackknives, and bowie knives. He pictured Pap sitting at a cornhusking party, polishing a fancy, pearl-handled knife. When anyone asked, Pap would proudly tell him, "It's a gift from my son. My son the soldier."

Thrasher quickly dug in his pockets and pulled out the few dollars he had left from pay. He was glad he hadn't wasted it away on poker.

"Hey, Thrasher," called Tim. He was standing in the doorway, pointing up the street. "Doesn't Hazen look dandy?"

Thrasher looked. Across the street, uniformed men were lined up in front of a photograph studio. Hazen stood out in the red battle shirt and tall black boots that his sister Cordelia had sent him.

"He sure does," said Thrasher, chuckling. He turned back to the knives and pipes, but then an idea struck him. A picture of himself in uniform would be just the right present to send to Pap and M'am. Now that was something Pap could be proud of. For sure.

"Come on, Tim," he cried. "Let's get our pictures, too."

CHAPTER

10

LATER, THE Twenty-sixth Regiment encamped outside Richmond, stretching themselves out, hurly-burly, on the hills. Thrasher and Tim sat cross-legged outside their tent. Thrasher studied his photograph for what seemed like the thousandth time.

At first Thrasher had wished he had the money for an ambrotype like Tim's, instead of settling for the less expensive *cartes de visite*. But as soon as he saw his photograph, he felt sorry he had wasted what little money he had.

It was no use. No matter how many times he looked at the photograph, he saw the same old Thrasher Magee. Sorry-looking eyes. Smooth face with fewer whiskers than a catfish. Soft, glum mouth. Flat cap on an even flatter head. Baggy gray coat. Short, broad hands folded one atop the other.

He didn't look like a man at all: He looked like a boy wearing a man's uniform.

The photographer had been a gruff, short-tempered man who grunted orders as he pushed Thrasher into position. "Sit up straight. Eyes forward. Look here—at my hand. Don't blink till I say so. That's it. Hold it!"

Poof! The powder flamed, startling Thrasher. The photographer barked, "Next!"

"Are you sending your picture to your family?" asked Tim.

"Naw," said Thrasher abruptly. "I don't know why I even bothered."

"It can't be as bad as you say," said Tim. "Let me see."

Reluctantly, Thrasher exchanged pictures with Tim.

Thrasher stared at Tim's ambrotype. Tim looked so soldierly, with one hand grasping the handle of his knife and the other holding his pistol. His dark hair, firmly set chin, and deep eyes made him appear serious and mature. Still, something seemed odd, although for the life of him, Thrasher couldn't figure it out. Frowning, he studied the photograph closer.

"I imagine city fellers like you get your pictures taken all the time," he said.

"My mother has many family pictures, but none like

this. This one will surprise her." Tim handed Thrasher's photograph back. "Your family will be proud."

Thrasher grunted and stowed the picture away in his haversack. "I'll send it soon as I got a battle to tell about."

"Good idea," said Tim. "So will I."

A battle will change everything. Thrasher imagined his picture setting on M'am's tiny chest of drawers in her lean-to bedroom. Or maybe she'd set it out in the main room, where visitors might see it. Or, better yet, maybe Pap would carry it around in his shirt pocket and pull it out to show folks at Thrifts' store.

Tim stretched out. Using his haversack for a pillow, he lay back and pulled his cap over his eyes.

Curses and loud voices rose up from the neighboring Twiggs County campsite, several tents away. It had the sound of a fight. Thrasher stood to get a better look. A ring of men was forming, and in the middle he saw Baylor, holding a hickory-rail bat in his hands. "It don't have to be a whole game," Baylor was saying. "Just a few innings."

The Twiggs County men cursed some more. Someone tossed shoes at Baylor, and someone else threw a cookpot. It landed with a clang in the dirt, raising a cloud of dust.

Disgusted, Baylor pushed his way past and straggled

back to his own campsite. "Nobody wants to do nothing," said Baylor. He propped the makeshift bat against a vine-covered oak, next to the guns.

"Everybody's tired," said Tim. "It's time to take a rest."

Hazen came from behind his tent, carrying his red battle shirt and black boots. The shirt was wet. He hung the shirt to dry on a tree limb, then sat next to Tim and began to shine his boots. "We all need a battle," he said. "That would be the best rest."

Baylor crawled into their tent and came out with two burlap sacks. He tied them to his belt and grabbed his gun from the tree.

Thrasher waited to see if Tim was going to jump up and join Baylor the way he usually did, but he didn't. Thrasher lifted the edge of Tim's cap and peeked beneath. His eyes were closed. He was sound asleep.

"Hold on, Baylor," called Thrasher, reaching for his gun. "I'm coming."

THE WOODS FELT COOL and damp. It was good to be away from camp. Here, among the trees, a feller could think.

"Baylor," he said. "You see Tim's picture?"

"Sure did."

"Notice anything peculiar?"

"Nothing more than a New Orleans peculiar," said Baylor. "And that makes Tim a heap less peculiar than Hazen."

"You see Hazen's red battle shirt?"

"Sure did," Baylor snorted. "Now that's a shirt that says 'shoot me.'"

Baylor stopped at a thin but sturdy maple sapling. He pulled out his bowie knife and sawed at the base of the trunk until the tree snapped free. He trimmed the limbs and leaves, fashioning the sapling into a long, forked pole.

"Now we'll catch one of them Yankees slithering about here," Baylor said.

"Yankees!" said Thrasher. "In these woods?"

Baylor nodded. "You'll see."

Thrasher knew it couldn't be so, but he continued through the woods with Baylor.

Suddenly, Baylor stopped and pointed. A rattlesnake was basking in a leafy spot of sunshine. In a flash, Baylor pinned the snake's head to the ground with his pole. The snake squirmed and rattled loudly, but Baylor eased it into the sack. He tied the end. The sack whirred and swelled, then grew quiet.

"Yankee," said Baylor, his face shining with excitement. "Now all we need is a Rebel and we'll have ourselves a good fight."

Thrasher took the forked pole from Baylor. He knew as well as any swamper the sorts of places snakes liked to hide—in a warm pile of leaves, on warm rocks, or beneath fallen trees. Before long, he found a perfectly rotted tree stump.

With a heave, the boys pushed the stump over. A long, black-ringed king snake stared back at them.

Quickly, he thrust the forked pole, pinning the snake's head to the ground. He eased the bag around the snake.

He knotted the wriggling sack and held it out. "Got you, you Rebel!"

"WHAT DID YOU GET?" asked Tim when the boys returned to camp. "Rabbit? Squirrel?"

"Better," said Baylor, barely able to conceal his excitement.

Thrasher and Baylor carried the sacks over to a grassy clearing near a stand of birch trees. Baylor cupped his hands around his mouth and hollered, "Snake fight!"

Wade, Goodloe, Hazen, and several boys hurried over. They pushed into a ring around Baylor and Thrasher. Thrasher swelled with pride. All eyes were on him and Baylor.

Baylor untied the neck of the first sack and dropped it by the fire. Thrasher gave it a poke with his rifle.

The sack whirred and swelled as if it were taking a deep breath. Then it grew silent. When it breathed again, out slithered the biggity rattler.

"You two are mad," said Tim, stepping back.

The rattlesnake coiled itself and focused its shoebutton eyes on Tim.

"This here's a Union snake we found hiding in the underbrush," said Baylor. "He was lying low, trying to sneak up on us and steal our plans. What you got to say for yourself, you low-bellied Yankee?"

The air thickened with the rattler's musky smell and the staccato sound of its rattles.

Baylor nodded at Thrasher, whose heart was flapping like a fish out of water. He untied his sack and poked it with his rifle.

The king snake slid soundlessly out of the bag and into the center of the circle. "This here's a Rebel snake," said Thrasher. "And he don't appreciate no Yankee slithering about our camp. Ain't that right, Reb?"

The king smiled as he tasted the air with his tongue. He turned slowly in the direction of the rattlesnake.

The rattler struck a beeline for the tall grass on the other side of the trees. It had nearly escaped when the king snake leaped and darted after the rattler.

He caught up. The two snakes writhed and twisted in the grass.

Wade and the others closed in, jostling each other as they pushed for better positions. They cheered and shouted as the rattler jumped and hissed and struck at the king snake. The rattler sank its teeth into the black-ringed body, but the king snake only smiled and began to coil himself around the rattler.

"Hooray!" shouted Wade.

The rattler twisted, and the two snakes rolled over and over, a mass of coils. Slowly, the king snake wrapped himself higher and tighter around the rattler until, at last, the rattler stopped writhing. In moments, the rattler hung limply inside the king's coils, dead from suffocation.

But for the king snake, it wasn't victory enough. He loosened his hold on the dead snake. Directly, he gripped the dead rattler's head in his mouth and began to swallow him.

"That's how it'll be with them Yankees," predicted Wade. "Their troops may be larger and have more poison, but size won't matter in a fight. We'll lick 'em. By God, we'll lick 'em."

Goodloe shook his head sadly. "I hope the war doesn't end like a snake fight. Surely a man can still have his pride without swallowing another man up."

CHAPTER

11

NEW ORDERS CAME DOWN the next morning. The troops were headed for Port Republic. There, Major Wilmot promised, they would meet up with Jackson. Together they would chase the Yankees from the South.

Their spirits high, the men whistled and joked as they rolled blankets, folded tents, packed haversacks, and cooked rations.

"Just wait," Wade told Thrasher as they crowded onto the train. "Those Yanks'll see that swampers ain't no ordinary men. We can out-track, out-hunt, and out-shoot any Bluebelly."

The skinny-necked boy from Twiggs County agreed. "It'll be a shame to even call it a fair fight."

"I hear some Yankees wear metal breastplates into battle," said another man. "To protect themselves."

"Cowards," said Hazen.

"I don't care what kind of fancy trumpery those Yankees got," said Baylor. He ran his fingers up and down the barrel of his gun. "I've had this-here musket ever since it was a pistol. It'll suit me just fine."

As the train crawled across the Virginia countryside, chugging past great barns and rich fields and over mountains and creeks, Thrasher thought about what Wade had said. *It's true. Swampers ain't no ordinary men. We settle our scores. We draw out our enemies, hack their spines, and fry up their tails with butter.*

BUT THE GREAT GENERAL Jackson didn't wait for the Georgians.

By the time Thrasher and the others arrived at Port Republic, a ferocious battle had already been fought. Jackson had routed the Yankees after hours of heavy fighting. Now Jackson and his troops were off chasing the Yankees from Virginia, sending them back up North where they belonged.

All that was left for the Twenty-sixth Georgia to do was bury the dead.

That morning, Thrasher stood, looking over the battlefield, as a gray mist slowly retreated through shattered trees. It reminded him of an early morning in the swamp, before the mist burned off.

But then the fog lifted, and he saw that the field was studded with bodies. Black flies buzzed everywhere, on dead Yankees and Rebels alike. They swarmed over blood-clotted holes in blue and gray uniforms, bloody faces, staring eyes, and mouths locked in final screams.

Buzzards circled and swooped over the fields.

Wade picked up a rock and chucked it hard at two huge buzzards that were pecking at the bloated body of a dead horse. The rock smacked the horse. The buzzards flapped their wings and protested loudly but stayed put. One dipped its beak into the horse's eye.

"Why couldn't Jackson have waited?" asked Hazen.

It was a stupid question, one nobody bothered to answer.

Thrasher took his hat off and wiped his forehead.

Goodloe rubbed his nose and stamped his feet. "We'd better get to work," he said. He started down the field.

Thrasher followed. He stood over the first body, a man about Wade's age. He knew what he had to do, but still he hesitated, afraid to touch the dead man. The bloody face, staring eyes, flies flitting in and out of the mouth, and the steamy cloud of putrid odor—it reminded him of the thick smell of greasy entrails of a gutted deer or bear.

An immense sadness filled Thrasher. He wondered about this man. What were his last thoughts? Did he have time to call out, to ask for help, to remember his wife and children? Was there a dog waiting for him back home?

Thrasher's throat hurt, too tight to swallow. Someone touched his shoulder, startling him.

He gulped and jerked away, then saw it was Tim. He braced himself, expecting Tim to make fun of his tears.

"You're not the only one," said Tim hoarsely. His eyes were red. "Look."

Wade had covered his face with his hands. Goodloe's eyes were closed, and his lips were moving in prayer. Hazen was pale as a ghost. Baylor was wiping his nose on his sleeve.

Thrasher blinked and rubbed his face with his shirt. He squared his shoulders and adjusted his cap. He knew about this, he had done it before, back home, for Pap—each time he'd gutted a deer, butchered a hog, wrung a chicken's neck, or drowned a litter of kittens.

The trick would be the same: remove himself from what he was doing, pretend they weren't his fingers, his hands.

"Let's get busy," he said gruffly to Tim.

· · · · ·

THRASHER LET HIS breathing go shallow until he floated somewhere above the battlefield. Down below, he and the others searched the pockets on body after body. They took out gold pocketwatches, packs of playing cards, letters tied with pretty ribbons, testaments, and photographs of women and children. A good number of the dead Rebels were boys, boys like Baylor and Tim.

They marked the belongings and set them aside to be sent home. The food, though—biscuits and dried beef—they wrapped inside their kerchiefs. They stuffed them into their haversacks for later, when their stomachs might allow them to eat again.

Thrasher blocked out everything he could: the smell, the sound, the sight of body after body. He and Tim carried them to huge graves that other men were digging. Inside the graves, other dead Rebels were lined up, shoulder to shoulder, like huge, bloated seeds.

And he hated the Yankees for making it necessary.

Here and there, they passed details of Yankees, also burying their dead. Thrasher found himself burning with an anger he had never felt before. Not even toward Pap.

When the last Rebel was buried, Thrasher stood and stared at the mountains. Somewhere beyond them, he knew, were Jackson's troops, and somewhere beyond that were the Yankees.

He wished he had wings and could fly over the graves and shattered trees, past the mountains, clear to Jackson and his army. He'd help them settle the score with the Yankees. He'd make sure the Yankees paid for what they had done here, for what they were doing to the South. He'd make sure they'd never want to set foot in the South again.

THAT NIGHT, under a sky heavy with stars, Thrasher and the others stood picket duty along the North River. They talked in solemn, hushed voices as they passed around the crackers, meat, and cheese they had collected from the pockets of the dead men. They tried to draw Thrasher in, but he didn't feel like talking or eating. He was still too angry.

Wade was sitting by Goodloe and Hazen. "I've been thinking on my boys," he said. "I hope Wade Junior's taking good care of his momma."

"I'm sure he is," said Goodloe. "You've got a fine family."

"Also been thinking on Wade Junior's right arm," said Wade. "That boy can sure fight. I reckon it's on account of that arm not being christened."

"His arm isn't christened?" asked Goodloe.

"I held it out of the baptizing water so it would pack a devil of a wallop when he got old enough." Wade paused, then added, "But now, I reckon that my boy's arm ought to be christened like the rest of him." He looked at Goodloe. "Maybe you could do the honor."

"It would be my pleasure," Goodloe said with a chuckle. "When I get home, the first thing I'm going to do is marry Miss Mary Joyce. The first time I laid eyes on her, I knew she was the wife for me. I would have married her before I left, except the Bible says that when a husband hath married a new wife, he shall not go to war for one year, but remain at home and cheer her up. The Good Lord willing, I'll cheer her up plenty when I return home."

Wade turned to Hazen. "How about you? Got any plans?"

"Promise you won't make fun?" asked Hazen.

Wade crossed his heart.

"I'd like to raise foxhounds. There's nothing in the world happier than a hound. And prideful! When I was a boy, I had a hound that would only give me two shots. If I missed on the second shot, that dog went home, embarrassed." Hazen looked over at Thrasher. "Everyone knows your Chum is the finest hunter around. Maybe you could give me some pointers."

Hazen's asking me? "I'd like nothing better," said

Thrasher. He felt even better than when he and Baylor'd had the snake fight.

Baylor was telling Tim about a sight of gators he had once seen in the swamp. "A hundred of them, at least," Baylor said. "What a racket! The water was a-churning as they was catching perch. And here's the funny part. A gator's tail would stick out of the water, and another gator'd be chomped onto it. They thought the tails was fish!"

Tim was laughing and shaking his head.

Baylor held out a bit of dried beef to Thrasher. "Hungry?"

"Naw." Thrasher shook his head. Behind him, in the darkness, a few cookfires still glittered, and somewhere there was singing, as if today had been no different than any other day.

All around him, nightsongs filled the shadows—chirrups and twitterings and the flutter of wings. From the river, a catfish jumped, and the splash carried Thrasher back home.

He slapped a mosquito off his cheek and wondered what M'am and the girls were doing. Did M'am give birth to the baby yet? Were Mabel, Rebecca, and Rosalie sitting on the porch, listening to the night sounds just as he was doing here? Was Pap up and about yet?

"This time back home," Wade was saying, "me and the boys would be strike fishing by the light of a pine-knot torch."

"Good time of year to fish," said Goodloe. "All a patient man has to do is hold out a net, and before long his net is full."

There were more splashes, nearer this time. *Catfish sure are jumpy,* thought Thrasher. But something was off about the splashes. They weren't silvery as they ought to be if they were coming from a catfish. No, they sounded more hollow and gurgly in a flat sort of way. It reminded him of poling through the swamp.

Poling. That's it. Thrasher's heartbeat quickened as he looked at the others, but no one else had heard the sound.

"Hush," he said.

The others fell silent, wary now. Their eyes searched his as they listened.

Thrasher gripped his rifle tighter. Was it a no-account Yankee prowling about, laying plans for a skirmish? If it was, he had to fire his gun to warn the rest of the regiment.

Or to kill a man.

He listened hard. Images of all the bodies they had buried that day raced through his mind. *If it's a no-account*

Yankee, why, I'll shoot him with nary a second thought. The Scriptures say to forgive your enemies, but I'll forgive with more grace after I get even.

Seconds passed. The noise came again. This time he knew for sure that it was no catfish. It came from a pole, being pushed against a river bottom. Nothing else could cause that hollow gurgle.

"Poling," he whispered, and he gripped his gun tighter.

Baylor's eyes met his, telling him he was right. Thrasher stuck his chin out stubbornly. He had heard the noise; that made it his call, whether to shout out or to fire his gun. He trained his gun in the direction of the noise and waited.

12

THE SECONDS STRETCHED intolerably until Thrasher finally heard the scrape of wood against dirt and stone.

"Halt!" he demanded, trying to keep the jump out of his trigger finger. "Who comes there?"

There was a rustling, then nothing. Finally a reply came from behind a bush. "Don't shoot, Rebel. We come in peace."

"Yankees," whispered Tim.

"Hush," said Baylor.

Everyone stood stone still. "Tell them to show themselves," said Hazen.

"I know what to say," hissed Thrasher. Then, a little louder, his voice shaky, he said, "Show yourselves." He squinted into the shadows.

"Not until we have an agreement," said the Yankee. "We've got a truce flag. We've also got one of your wounded."

"It's a trick," warned Hazen.

Thrasher chewed his lip. He knew Yankees couldn't be trusted. He thought of the bloodied faces and piles of bodies. He had seen what Yankees could do.

"We've got our sights on you Yanks," warned Thrasher. "Step out so we can see your hands above your head."

"We'd like to oblige you, but we can't," said the Yankee. "Our hands are full. With one of your own — a Rebel."

"Not that he weighs much," said a second Yankee voice. "You Rebs must be as low on food as you are on ammunition."

The Yankees' sass riled up Hazen. "What makes you think we're low on ammunition?"

"You fellas always wait until we're real close before you shoot," said the Yankee. The voice was teasing in a friendly way.

"Of course," said the first voice. "Maybe that's because of those sticks you Rebels call rifles."

"They got awful smart mouths for Yanks behind Rebel lines," Wade told Thrasher.

Thrasher agreed. Those Yankees sure had sass. "You're wearing my patience mighty thin, Yanks. I'll say it once more before I shoot: Step out where we can see you."

"Hold on, Reb." There was fumbling and the clatter of metal against metal. The two voices were arguing. "Go ahead," said one. "Stick that flag out where they can see."

"Don't push me," said the other. "Do you want to go first?"

The bushes rustled some more, and then a truce flag—a pair of dingy white drawers tied to a stick—poked out from behind the branches. The two men stepped out of the shadows. They were carrying a moaning Rebel on a makeshift stretcher.

Goodloe and Tim knelt by the Rebel's side. The man's eyes fluttered weakly. Tim loosened the man's shirt, then gasped at his glistening intestines. Goodloe turned his head, his lips whispering a prayer.

Thrasher knew a belly wound was the worst to have. Couldn't amputate it like an arm or a leg and couldn't do much to stave off the infection that 'most always set in.

Still, it made him suspicious. Why would these two Yankees go to so much trouble to return a Rebel so close to death? He gripped his gun even tighter.

· · · · ·

NOW THAT THE YANKEES were closer, Thrasher could make out their faces in the moonlight. The taller Yank had a boyish face like Tim's. The second Yank was shorter and older. He had a beard that stuck out, reminding Thrasher of a picture he'd seen of a lion.

Lion Beard spoke first. "I know it must look awful crazy to return this here Reb. But it didn't seem Christian to let him die among strangers or alone in the woods where we found him."

The tall Yank with the smart mouth nodded in agreement. "There's just our company left on burial duty. The other sixty thousand send their apologies for their hasty departure."

"If y'all need any help burying your dead, let us know," said Baylor. "We're happy to bury as many as we can."

Tall Yank chuckled at Baylor. "The pleasure goes both ways." He elbowed Lion Beard. "Hey, Cousin, looks like we've met a school of fresh fish here."

"Fresh fish!" said Hazen.

"Your uniforms match," said Lion Beard. "Your regiment hasn't fought yet, has it?"

Thrasher looked closely at the Yankees' uniforms. Even in the darkness, he could see that their blue coats were of different cut and design, patched and frayed. Tall Yank's sleeves ended inches above his wrists. Lion

Beard's pant legs were hiked up around his shins. Their hats didn't match either.

"We wanted to fight!" said Hazen. "Jackson started without us."

"He finished without you, too," said Tall Yank.

Behind them, the wounded Rebel moaned. "Wa—ter."

Tim took off his jacket, bundled it, and slid it under the man's head. Goodloe lifted his canteen to the man's cracked lips. The water dribbled down the side of his face. Tim gently swabbed the water with a dirty handkerchief.

"Just make him comfortable," whispered Tim to Goodloe. "It's all we can do."

"Let—ter," said the man. "Wife . . . chil—dren . . . home."

Tim reached inside the man's coat pocket. He took out a folded letter. "I'll send it home," said Tim. "Don't you worry. We'll take care of everything."

"Bless . . . you," said the man. His eyes fluttered some more, and his chest rattled for air.

Tim and Goodloe squatted by the man, tending him, watching over him.

"The Lord is my shepherd," Goodloe began. "I shall not want."

"He maketh me lie down in green pastures," said

Tim. "He leadeth me beside still waters; He restoreth my soul. He leadeth me in the paths of righteousness for His name's sake."

The words comforted Thrasher. The still waters and green pastures reminded him of home—slow-moving waterways, gentle prairie heads, floating islands.

Lion Beard removed his cap. "Yea, though I walk through the valley of the shadow of death," he said, "I fear no evil; for Thou art with me; Thy rod and thy staff, they comfort me."

Thrasher glanced around. Tall Yank was moving his lips, and Wade and Hazen were, too, their voices blending together just like in church. "Thou preparest a table before me in the presence of mine enemies," they prayed together. "Thou annointest my head with oil, my cup overfloweth."

It hit Thrasher, all of a sudden, how odd it was. The Yankees and Rebels spoke the same language, knew the same prayers, prayed to the same God.

"Surely goodness and mercy shall follow me all the days of my life," they said. "And I shall dwell in the house of the Lord forever. Amen."

Goodloe pointed to the johnnycakes lying on his haversack. "I suppose this might be the Lord's table in the presence of our enemies."

He picked up the cakes and weighed them in his

hands, as if he were weighing an idea. "You Yanks committed a moral act of goodness and mercy when you returned our fallen comrade," he said.

He nodded at the white drawers hanging from the stick. "And seeing your truce flag—" He paused, looked around at the others, then back at the Yankees. "Let's call off this cruel war for a spell."

Of all the harebrained notions! "You can't call off a war!" Thrasher said sharply.

Goodloe seemed embarrassed. "Pardon our young friend here. He's forgotten his manners."

"Have not!"

"He's even forgotten he's forgotten them," said Goodloe.

A hint of a smile creased Tall Yank's face, and the sass left his voice. "War makes everyone forget."

"It's a truce, then," said Goodloe. "Till midnight?"

The Yanks looked at each other and nodded.

Thrasher couldn't believe it. Goodloe must be touched in the head. Prayer or no prayer, God or no God, had Goodloe forgotten the bloated bodies they had buried? The letters that had to be sent home to children and wives and mothers? Thrasher would *never* forget the sight, not if he lived to be a hundred.

"What we ought to do," said Thrasher, "is shoot these Yankees. It'll make two less to shoot later."

. . . . .

GOODLOE IGNORED Thrasher and handed the johnnycakes to the Yankees. In seconds, the food was gone.

"Let's drink to our truce," said Lion Beard. He brought out a good-sized flask, took a swig, then offered it to Thrasher. "You're awful quiet, son."

"I ain't your son," said Thrasher, pushing the flask away. "And I ain't taking nothing from no Yankee—lest it's a dead one."

"Too bad," said Lion Beard. "It's not the first time Yanks and Rebs truced together. Why, me and my cousin have sneaked across picket lines to play cards with Rebels." He grinned. "Of course we beat them every time."

"We even went swimming together," said Lion Beard. "Once outside Richmond, we held a swimming party with a whole bunch of Rebs."

"I reckon there ain't nothing uglier than a white-bellied Yankee," said Thrasher. "Lest it's a Bluebellied one."

Everyone laughed, which startled Thrasher. He blinked, unsure of himself. He didn't intend the words as a joke, yet the men had laughed. Even the Yankees.

"Good one," said Baylor. He raised the whiskey flask

in salute to Thrasher, then took a swallow and passed the flask on.

The lion-bearded Yankee looked at Goodloe. "I don't suppose you have any tobacco. I always enjoy tobacco after a good meal."

"That so?" said Goodloe with a nod. "I always enjoy coffee."

"I have coffee," said Lion Beard.

"You do?" Goodloe's face lit up. He nudged Baylor with his elbow. "Give him some tobacco."

Baylor fished in his pocket for a plug. He bit off a piece for himself, then handed the rest to the Yankee. In return, Lion Beard gave Goodloe a small pouch. Goodloe opened it and inhaled its contents deeply. "Real, honest-to-goodness coffee," he said with a sigh.

"Maybe you fellers are human after all," said Wade.

Lion Beard grunted. With his knife, he hacked at the tobacco plug. He handed half to his buddy.

"What else might you have?" asked Goodloe. "Any newspapers?"

Thrasher gripped his gun. *Stop!* he wanted to yell. *This is crazy talk. Y'all are swapping and joking like y'all just met fishing.*

The tall Yank dug beneath his jacket and brought out a worn newspaper. "Just our camp newspaper." He pointed to an article on the front page. "I wrote that one myself, about one of our baseball games."

"Baseball?" said Baylor. "Y'all any good?"

Tall Yank nodded. "We beat the officers in that game."

Goodloe took the newspaper and looked it over. "The *Pennsylvania Thirteenth*," he said, squinting at the masthead.

"Potter County," said Lion Beard. "My cousin Bill and me and about three hundred other boys floated down the Susquehanna on rafts, all the way to Harrisburg. It took us the better part of three days."

"How about you fellas?" asked Lion Beard.

"The Twenty-sixth Georgia," said Wade. "Charlton County. The Okefinokee Rifles."

"I lived in Pennsylvania, once, a long time ago," said Goodloe. "With my Jenkin cousins, near Scranton. They're fighting with the Forty-eighth."

"Well, well," said Lion Beard. "So you have Yankee cousins. I knew there was goodness about you." He eyed Goodloe curiously. "Why'd you leave Scranton?"

"Georgia is my home. Always has been."

"Home," said Lion Beard. There was a longing in his voice. "I've been so hungry for my wife's pasty. She makes this pasty—it's a pie with steak and potatoes and onions inside."

"My littlest girl turned two years old yesterday," said

Tall Yank. "I doubt if she even remembers me. I'll be a stranger to her when I get home."

"Let's drink to home," said Goodloe. "To wives and sweethearts, children and dogs."

The flask made another round. Thrasher could tell from the way they were all swallowing hard and studying their fingertips that a wave of homesickness had soaked them all. It was too long for them all to be away from loved ones and dogs and crops.

THE FLASK had made three more rounds when Lion Beard said suddenly, "If it were up to us, I'll bet we could have this war settled in a matter of minutes."

More crazy talk, thought Thrasher.

"Oh?" said Hazen briskly. "And just what would you Yankees suggest?"

"Every Reb I meet says the same thing," said Lion Beard. "You're fighting for your rights. Rights for what, I want to know? Nearly every one of you is a poor cracker."

"Ain't nothing wrong with being poor," said Thrasher.

"I'm not saying there's anything wrong with it," said Lion Beard. "It's the same with my cousin and me. We're nothing but poor farmers. Poor before the war and poor after the war."

"Maybe even poorer," said Tall Yank.

"The North thinks we're fighting for slaves," said Goodloe. "But most of us don't even own slaves."

"That's what makes me think that this is a rich man's war," said Lion Beard. "You fellas aren't fighting to preserve slavery. And me and my cousin here aren't fighting to free them."

"Then why are you fighting?" asked Wade.

"My great-grandfather fought in the Revolution," Lion Beard said proudly. "I'm not going to let this country go to ruin."

"It's our duty," said Tall Yank.

"We got duty, too," said Thrasher, annoyed. He looked at Goodloe earnestly. Goodloe always had the right words. He would know what to say. "Tell them, Goodloe. Tell them about all our rights."

"What rights might they be, my young friend?" Lion Beard asked Thrasher solemnly.

Thrasher fumbled for words as he tried to think of a few hardy rights. Finally, he said, "Whatever rights we got that you Yankees want to take from us."

Lion Beard and Tall Yank shook their heads sadly.

Suddenly Baylor popped to his feet. "I reckon there's a way to decide this war once and for all." His eyes were shining, the way they did when he was up to something.

Lion Beard's eyes narrowed. "How's that?"

"Baseball," said Baylor.

The tall Yank's eyes lit up. "Baseball?"

Hazen stared in disbelief. "Baylor, what in the blazes do you think you're doing?"

"You're crazier than these Yankees," said Thrasher.

But Wade agreed with Baylor. "Why not?"

"Baseball's a good idea," said Goodloe. "Not crazy at all."

The two Yankees stood aside and talked it over between themselves, then turned to the Rebels. "If you give your word you'll be fair," said Lion Beard, "we'll pick six to match your six here and meet you tomorrow in the clearing beyond your camp. It'll be No Man's Land."

"No Man's Land it is," said Baylor, pumping Lion Beard's hand. "You got our word. We'll give you Bluebellies the best whupping you ever got."

"We'll fry you fresh fish," joked Tall Yank.

Behind them, Tim stood slowly and took off his cap. The wounded man's chest was still at last. Blood trickled from his mouth.

All of them, Rebel and Yankee alike, removed their caps and bowed their heads in silent prayer.

13

THE NEXT DAY, in a clearing, the white flag fluttered from a pole planted between the Rebel and Yankee teams. No Man's Land. Two rocks, a haversack, and a rotted stump marked the bases.

From his position in the outfield, Thrasher looked at Lion Beard, who was swinging a hickory-rail bat in warm-up circles over his head. Four other straggly-looking Yankees milled about the sidelines, stamping their feet and stretching their arms and legs. Like the first two Yanks, they wore mismatched jackets and shirts, some short in the sleeves, some short in the pants, patch upon patch, and muddy.

Goodloe was pitching. He wound up and chucked the yarn ball toward the tall Yank. The Yank swung the hickory rail, smacking the yarn ball. It sailed deep toward Baylor.

The Rebels whooped.

"Baylor! It's yours!" hollered Thrasher. Last night the game had sounded like a ridiculous idea. But now, his heart beat fast. This was no ordinary game, one on a side. This was his chance—their chance—to show those Yankees who was going to win this war after all.

Baylor ran toward the ball and scooped it up.

Cheers rose up from the Yankees as the tall Yank dug for first base and churned.

Baylor aimed for the Yank. Too late: Tall Yank was safe at the rotted stump that marked second base. He flashed a grin like an alligator showing off his teeth.

"Fresh fish!" hollered the Yankees.

Baylor spit. "That's all right," he shouted, tossing the ball back to Goodloe. "You ain't never making it home."

"We got your scent now," said Wade. "We ain't throwing off your trail till we got y'all treed."

By the time it was Thrasher's turn to bat, the Rebels had four runs to the Yankees' eight. The Yankee pitcher tossed the ball toward Thrasher. It wobbled. Thrasher swung and smacked it hard. He could hear the Rebels cheer as he rounded first and sped on to second.

"Run! Run!" shouted Hazen, waving him on.

The rotted tree stump was within easy reach when the ball hit him, square in the seat of the pants.

"Out!" shouted the Yankees. A harmonica sang out "Yankee Doodle."

"They soaked you," said Tim. "Are you all right?"

Thrasher nodded. His backside stung, but his disappointment smarted even more. "I'll get them. Next time I'm making it all the way home."

WHEN IT WAS Thrasher's turn to bat again, the score was tied at ten. Hazen was on third base; Baylor was sitting on the stump at second; Wade stood at first.

Both sides groaned when they saw that Wade's hit had reduced the yarn ball to a pile of thread, and the minie ball was lost in the grass.

"Find a rock," shouted a Yankee.

The Rebels and the Yanks scoured the field.

"Here, Yank," said Tim. He tossed a walnut-sized rock to the Yankee pitcher.

The Yankee wadded the unraveled yarn around the rock, but it was still a sorry sight. "We need something more," he said.

Wade nudged Hazen. "Give him one of your socks. You're the only one with a spare pair."

Grumbling, Hazen peeled off his sock and handed it

to the Yankee, who dropped the yarn-and-rock wadding into it. He packed the sock tightly, then stretched and knotted the end. Cheering, the teams fell back into their places.

Thrasher planted his feet and locked his eyes on the Yankee pitcher. It felt as if the fate of the Confederacy rode on the game's outcome. *Come on, Yank,* he thought. *Pitch me a good one.*

He wanted to smack that sock ball past the outfield, over the battlefield, past the mountains, all the way into Jackson's camp, bringing every Rebel runner home.

The Yankee drew back his arm, ready to throw. But before he could, the Rebel bugle flared. The Georgians were called to formation.

Thrasher lowered the hickory rail. He blinked in disbelief and disappointment.

Wade, Baylor, and Tim started to run across from the field. Wade turned and hollered, "Hurry up."

Goodloe took the truce flag down. He stood there, staring at the white drawers in his hands.

"You all right?" asked Thrasher.

Goodloe didn't answer right away. But then he said, "These plain cotton drawers were powerful enough to hold peace between two armies."

He looked back at the woods, where the Yankees

were walking across the opposite end of the field. They were a flash of faded blue, slipping between the trees.

Goodloe wiped his hands over his face, then drew himself up. He straightened his shirt and adjusted his glasses. "Come on," he said to Thrasher. "Let's go find out which direction the war is headed."

Thrasher looked back at the woods one last time. No more blue showed between the trees. The Yankees were gone.

ONCE AGAIN, they struck camp. Thrasher and the rest of the Rebels moved out, thousands of gray-clad men, across the Virginia mountains, creeks, and rivers in an attempt to catch Jackson.

At first Thrasher replayed the baseball game in his head. If only he had gotten the chance to smack that ball. He couldn't stop thinking about it. As the men marched, clouds of dust sifted into his hair, his eyes, every inch of him.

Then it began to rain. In the beginning, it was a soft rain that melted against Thrasher's face and dampened his hat and jacket. It smelled like the rain back home, clean and good, and Thrasher thought of the many times he had fished in the rain. Fish were always biting then.

But the rain didn't stop. Soon thousands of feet churned the wet roads into mud so deep, it swallowed men's shoes. Thrasher took off his shoes. He tied them together and hung them around his neck. His feet ached. *In wartime,* he thought, *you make do. Far better to march barefoot than to lose shoes altogether.*

Buzzards circled and dipped in the air, and he thought about the bodies he had buried at Port Republic. It was ugly, but he had done his duty.

He thought about the night on picket duty when the Yankees came a-calling. He had detected the sound of the pole. He had trained his gun on them. He had done his duty then, too.

Is this what it means to be a man? he wondered.

It rained still more. Orders were given to cut tall pines to corduroy the roads. This way, wagons and artillery could pass through without becoming hopelessly mired in mud.

The men stopped marching and started cutting the trees. All around in the forest, the smell of fresh pine filled the air as axes rang out, and tall pines crashed.

Thrasher rested his ax on a tree stump. He looked at his hands, cracked and blistered. If he were home, M'am would slather goose grease on them and wrap them with soft cloths.

"Do you think we'll ever get there?" asked Hazen. His voice was tired. He brushed at the pine chips sticking to his hat and shirt. For the first time, Thrasher noticed how much weight Hazen had lost.

"Get where?" growled Wade. He set his ax down. His back bones crackled as he straightened. "Don't even know where we're going." He sneezed violently several times, then wiped his nose on his sleeve. His nose had been runny for several days now. His eyes were red and wild-looking.

Goodloe's glasses were splattered with mud. He took them off, huffed on them, and wiped at the mud. "And when we do get there," he said, fitting his glasses, now hopelessly smeared, over his ears, "it's always someplace else we're going."

"I hear Robert E. Lee's replacing General Joe Johnston," said Tim. He took off his cap and wiped the sweat from his brow. His eyes were dark hollows in his face.

There was more grumbling. This was not good news, as far as Thrasher and the others were concerned. How could someone nicknamed Granny Lee ever replace fighting Joe Johnston? They had lost a valiant leader when Johnston fell at Seven Pines.

It rained still more, and they marched again.

War wasn't anything like Thrasher had imagined.

His legs ached, his feet blistered, and his stomach sassed him. With each step, he wondered how he could have been such a fool as to ever join up. He wished he was home again, patching the henhouse, or chinking the log walls, or doing any of the chores he used to complain about. He longed for his bed, for Chum, for the warmth of home and M'am's cooking, even for his sisters' teasings.

"I don't mind marching," said Hazen. "As long as there's fighting at the end of it."

Wade spun around and gave Hazen a shove in the chest. "Keep off my feet," he growled. "You march like a cow."

THE RIVERS RAGED and tore away bridges and swept away supplies, and the men cut still more trees and built more bridges.

Supplies were running low, and rations were cut in half. The meat now included so many shanks and necks that Baylor joked how the cook would be serving up the hooves and horns next.

Still, as hungry and tired as Thrasher was, there was nothing he hungered for more than a glimpse of Stonewall Jackson. If he could see the general, then the marching, the blisters, the hunger would be worth it.

He imagined the general seeking him out, asking

him his opinion on the war, his plan for a battle. Thrasher would salute the general, but not in the grand manner Hazen would. A simple, snappy salute.

He'd introduce the general to the Okefinokee Riflers. "General," he'd say, "these are the finest, fightingest men to come out of Charlton County. We'll make the South safe again. We'll see to it. You can count on us."

As the days wore on, he searched the ragged columns of men for the general. All he saw were bleary eyes and gaunt, tired faces. He listened for the general's voice. But all he heard was the clink of metal against metal and the beat of drums.

Jackson was nowhere to be found.

Swirls of reports each placed the general in a different place—here on his sorrel horse, there riding a train to Richmond, or somewhere in disguise in between, always tricking the Yankees.

Jackson, Thrasher decided, was like the gray mist that crept through the Okefinokee—always present but always beyond his grasp.

14

THE RAIN STOPPED, but gray was everywhere—the mist, the fog, the skies. For several more days, the Georgians plodded from hill to hill, with soldiers so tired and numb, they blindly followed the feet in front of them. At night, they bivouacked without tents, snatching only a bit of sleep. Then they marched again.

Late one afternoon, they came to a crossroads marked by horse tracks. Word spread through the ranks that cavalry had passed through the area.

"Maybe it's Jeb Stuart and his men!" Thrasher was hopeful as they marched through. "Maybe they're on a spy mission."

Goodloe grunted in agreement. "Stuart loves to ride

circles around the enemy, steal supplies and equipment, then read about himself in the newspaper."

How grand it sounded. Thrasher turned to tell Baylor, but he was nowhere in sight.

"Where's Baylor?" he asked.

Tim shifted his haversack to his other shoulder and grunted. "He's been missing all day."

"I hope he's all right," said Thrasher. He was beginning to worry now. He hadn't seen Baylor since early morning, when Baylor had slipped from ranks to pick green ears of corn for roasting.

"Baylor's always all right," said Tim. "He hasn't a care in the world."

"How can he be that-away?" said Thrasher crossly. "He's got to be as hungry and tired and wet as the rest of us."

"That's the way some men are," said Tim, and Thrasher could tell Tim was brooding, too. "Growing up doesn't come with age. It comes with accepting your responsibility. My mother always told me that there are men who are fourteen and boys who are forty."

Men who are fourteen. He glanced quickly at Tim, trying to read his face.

Tim nodded, smiling. "Yes, I'd say you're a man who's fourteen."

Embarrassed now, Thrasher looked away. He thought

of how, in the beginning, Tim had seemed too uppity to be an Okefinokee Rifler. But now, Tim was just like one of them. He felt lucky to have a friend like Tim.

A man who's fourteen. As tired as Thrasher was, he squared his shoulders and straightened his back.

THE REGIMENT WAS TOLD to step it up, to close up the ranks that had grown too long and straggly. Baylor, dirty but happy, mysteriously reappeared, like a cat at feeding time. He fell into step alongside Thrasher and Tim. "Y'all will never guess what I saw."

Thrasher didn't answer.

"A mule—buried clean up to its ears in mud. "'Course, it was a rather small mule." Baylor waited expectantly for a laugh.

Thrasher was in no mood for jokes. He shifted his haversack and bedroll to relieve his sore shoulders. "When are you ever going to learn, Baylor? A soldier's got his duty to do. He can't just take off like that."

Baylor swallowed hard and tried again. "I would've been here sooner. Except the mud swallered up my shoes and I had to dig a foot to find them." He punched Thrasher playfully on the shoulder.

Thrasher felt like popping Baylor a good one in the nose, but he resisted the urge. Instead, he snapped, "You ain't never going to make a real soldier."

Baylor refused to let up. "Why, Thrasher, if I start doing my duty now, I'll be all dutied out by the time a fight comes along. What kind of soldier would I make then?"

Thrasher failed to see anything worth joking about. The others—Goodloe, Hazen, Wade, Tim, and even Thrasher himself—had shaped into soldiers just fine. They acted as one group, one company, one army. They put duty first.

But not Baylor. Duty was just a word to Baylor, a word that meant nothing. Thrasher hated to admit it, but nothing bothered Baylor enough to change—not the bodies they buried, not the letters they sent home to the loved ones of dead soldiers, not the marching. Nothing.

Tim jumped in, exasperated. "Can't you see Thrasher's right? We've got to know we can *depend* on you."

Baylor's mouth dropped open, and his eyes widened. He seemed genuinely shocked. "'Course y'all can depend on me." He fumbled with the sack, opened it, held it out. "Looky here. I got us some sugar-cured pork and some apple butter and biscuits already slathered with jam from a farmer's wife. Hate to eat this all by myself."

Thrasher's mouth watered at the smell of the pork.

He couldn't remember when he'd last had a good meal. And the biscuits! They looked as flaky as M'am's. It was too much.

"No sense for our stomachs to hold a grudge," he told Tim. Forgiveness spread through him, warm and crispy.

THE MEN SLOGGED through two more days of mud, but on Sunday, the sun finally broke through the clouds. It felt cheerful and warm as it flooded through the steaming trees. The men filed into a clover field surrounded by piney woods and were ordered to pray.

"What's the use of praying?" whispered Thrasher to Tim. "It ain't prayer we need. We need food and a good night's sleep."

Tim closed his eyes and nodded tiredly.

Thrasher was tired, so tired he ached clear to the bone. If he shut his eyes for a second, he felt sure he would sleep for twenty years. He wondered what it would be like to wake up and find the war long over.

He glanced around the large circle of men, three and four deep, who had removed their hats. He took in their ragged uniforms, hollow cheeks, red-rimmed eyes, stubbled faces, and straggly hair. If he woke up in twenty years, who among them would be left? Who would be rocking on porches, telling war stories to children and grandbabies?

He looked at Goodloe and imagined him preaching from the pulpit, and Miss Mary Joyce sitting in the front pew. He imagined Wade surrounded by a whole passel of grandbabies. He saw Tim and thought what a fine daddy he'd make some day. He looked at Baylor and wondered if he'd ever settle down long enough to marry.

Across from him, heads began to tip in the direction of a man who knelt apart from the rest, his body perfectly erect, his uniform and hat muddied, the buttons clipped from his coat.

A wave of elbows nudged each other. Whispers rippled from one barefooted, soggy man to the next. Their faces lit up, and they grinned.

Thrasher chewed his lip thoughtfully as he studied the man. There was something familiar about the probing eyes, sunken beneath an overhanging brow. Something familiar, indeed. He knew this face. He had seen it before, in pictures.

It was Jackson! General Thomas "Stonewall" Jackson!

Thrasher was so happy, he just about melted down as he watched Jackson pray. He stared at the general, carving each line, each hair indelibly in his memory. Inch by inch he took in the broad, open forehead, the long, straight nose, the thin, colorless cheeks, the dark rusty beard. This was a man like no other.

When Jackson opened his blue eyes and stood, it was subtle, so subtle you'd have to scratch for it, but Thrasher was sure the general had singled him out, caught his eye. In that second, Thrasher saw the hope that Jackson had for him. He knew what Jackson expected of him. He saw himself in battle, alongside Jackson, fighting the Yankees, driving the Yankees from the South.

He held the thought for a moment until it wavered and disappeared. Pap's face rose in its place. Pap's hands were reaching for him.

Thrasher shuddered, almost afraid to look at Jackson again. His arms and legs suddenly grew weak. He couldn't move. It was the same as back home, when he'd first fired the long rifle, when he'd stuck his first hog, when he'd stood at the gator hole, transfixed, unable to hack through the gator's spine.

What if he couldn't fight? What if he couldn't shoot someone who spoke his language, prayed to his God? What if he just stood there, mired in mud?

Or worse: What if he ran?

At that, all the pleasure of seeing Jackson slipped from Thrasher; suddenly, he needed to be anywhere but here in this clearing, on the same patch of earth with the famous general.

He stumbled away from the others and ran into the woods, not stopping until something clutched in his stomach. He doubled over in pain and retched in the leaves.

When he stopped heaving, Thrasher peeled the thin bark from a slender birch and chewed it to take away the sour taste. He leaned against the tree and pressed his hands to his face. His hands felt cold and clammy.

He thought about the days ahead of him. Something powerful lay there, beyond him. He felt it.

Yet, deep down he knew: It didn't matter how many miles he had marched, drills he had practiced, bodies he had buried, Yankees he had held at gunpoint. He was still the same boy, the same yellow-bellied boy who'd walked out of the swamp two months ago.

He hadn't changed at all.

Weak-kneed now, he squatted with his back against the tree. Was he the only one who felt this way? Goodloe and Hazen and Wade never talked about it. No one did.

Somewhere Thrasher heard twigs snapping and the soft sound of feet treading on damp leaves. He made out the gray uniform of a fellow Rebel. He squinted and saw that it was Tim. Alone.

Thrasher sat stone-still, hoping he blended into the trees. He didn't want Tim to see him here. Tim would know something was wrong.

Tim reached inside his jacket. He took out pieces of cloth and then unbuttoned his pants. Thrasher knew he should turn his head, but he couldn't help but look. Tim dropped his pants, and Thrasher stared as the pants bunched around Tim's feet; he stared as smooth white legs emerged, and there, farther up—

Thrasher's stare stopped there. He was shocked by what he saw, but he still stared.

Tim wasn't the same as Thrasher. Tim wasn't the same as any of them.

Tim was a girl.

15

THE PAST DAYS and weeks flashed in Thrasher's mind—Tim's insistence on sleeping on the outside, creeping off to the woods to change or do whatever, refusing to participate in their swimming parties.

Glory, thought Thrasher. *I been sleeping, dressing, soldiering next to a girl. A girl.*

Now everything about Tim seemed so obvious—his smooth face, slender fingers. Thrasher supposed he should say *her* hands, but it felt all wrong, shamefully wrong.

He looked back at Tim, who was standing now, buttoning her pants, done doing whatever a girl does in the woods. *Why would a girl do such a thing?* he wondered.

Why would a girl fit herself up like a man and join the army?

Slowly, Thrasher's bewilderment turned to anger as he watched Tim head back to the others. He felt as if a cruel joke had been played on him. Tim wasn't who Thrasher thought she was. Tim wasn't even *what* Thrasher thought she was.

THRASHER PICKED A SPOT between Baylor and Wade, a comfortable distance from Tim, who was bent over a book of poetry, reading aloud in turns with Goodloe. Thrasher wished he could concentrate on the poetry, but he couldn't quit stealing glances at Tim's pants and thinking about what he had seen there.

He knew his duty required him to report Tim. He had to tell somebody—Major Wilmot or one of the other officers. Somebody ought to know. Somebody had to know. But his feelings were all jumbled up, tripping and colliding in his head.

"Here's one of my favorite odes by Wordsworth," said Goodloe.

> Our birth is but a sleep and a forgetting:
> The soul that rises with us our life's Star,

Hath had elsewhere its setting,
And come from afar:
Not in entire forgetfulness,
And not in utter nakedness,
But trailing clouds of glory do we come
From God, who is our home.

"Trailing clouds of glory," repeated Tim. "Do you think we trail clouds of glory when we return home to God?"

"I plan on it," said Goodloe, nodding.

Thrasher eyed Tim curiously. Is that what Tim was fighting for? Clouds of glory?

He thought about all that he'd seen Tim do. Tim had marched alongside Thrasher, drilled alongside him, buried bodies alongside him. It was Tim whose strength Thrasher had grown to admire, Tim who'd called him a man of fourteen.

A man's character shows in his respect for his work. That's what Pap always said.

Thrasher shook his head. He couldn't think about all that now. Tim was a girl. That changed everything. *Besides, if you can't count on a person to be who he says he is, then how can you count on him at all?*

Who *she* says she is. He, she, him, her—oh, it was too much to sort through.

Baylor bit off a piece of hardtack and chewed vigorously. "If I run out of bullets tomorrow, I'm using hardtack." He offered a piece to Thrasher, who refused. "Y'all out of chat?" said Baylor.

"I got a load on my mind," said Thrasher. He stood and looked west to the mountains, where the evening sun was spreading, a ribbon of orange. He wondered what M'am and the girls were doing now, if they were looking at the same sunset and thinking about him.

At the neighboring campsite, Hazen was visiting the Twiggs County men. He was listening intently to a tall, bearded man. Hazen nodded his head, then ran back to Thrasher and the others.

"Have you heard?" said Hazen. "We've found a hole in the right flank of the Union army. Tomorrow will be a baptism of fire."

It was news that everyone had been waiting for, yet no one said a word. Goodloe and Tim looked away from the poetry book. Wade stared at his fingertips. Baylor concentrated on wiping the barrel of his musket.

Hazen seemed taken aback at the silence. "Isn't anyone going to say anything? Tomorrow we fight for our country's honor."

"Honor," said Wade, glooming. "What's honor?"

"Honor is standing up and declaring who you are,"

said Hazen. "Tomorrow we declare ourselves, just as Georgia did when she seceded from the Union."

"Will honor put food on my table? Raise my boys? Love my wife?" said Wade. He stood and stamped off into the woods.

The others watched Wade disappear. Goodloe drew in a deep breath. "The air smells clean and gentle. That's a good sign. I'm sure of it."

Baylor held out his gun. "The only sign I need is my Miss Daisy. She'll protect me."

"Daisy!" said Tim. "I thought you named your gun Olivia."

"I did before I met Miss Daisy." He cradled his gun in his arms. "What a sweet thing she is. A voice like a songbird."

Thrasher looked from Baylor, still sitting, hugging his gun, to Tim, who was also sitting, hugging her knees. *If only Baylor knew,* he thought. *All along he could've named his gun Tim.*

THRASHER LAY on the damp ground that night. They weren't permitted to use tents, for bivouac meant blankets only. He was grateful for the excuse not to sleep in a tent next to Tim.

He heard Goodloe's breathing, slow and steady, in

the darkness. Hazen was asleep, too. Wade was restless, tossing and turning.

Tim's a girl. The image haunted him — her pants bunched around her ankles. Her smooth white legs.

He tried to stop his thoughts there, but he couldn't. He rolled over and forced his thoughts to tomorrow's battle.

War. He imagined the hole in the right flank of the Union army.

Maybe they were the baseball Yankees.

He didn't want to think about the baseball Yankees out there.

He didn't want to think about Tim.

An ache slowly spread inside Thrasher. He wished more than anything that he were home, lying in the tiny cabin, so crowded with sisters that it was impossible for a feller to get a moment's peace.

He stared at the stars. It was late. Back home, they'd all be in bed: Pap sucking on his teeth; Mabel and Rebecca squawking over their share of the blanket; Rosalie sucking her thumb; M'am humming to the new baby; Chum, sleeping on the porch.

He wished he had the comfort of Chum now.

"Hey! Thrasher, Tim," whispered Baylor, "Y'all asleep?"

Thrasher felt relieved he wasn't the only one awake. "Naw," he said.

Baylor rolled onto his side. Even in the darkness, Thrasher could see him propped up on a skinny elbow. "I been thinking on how much my stomach would like some apple-butter muffins or scuppernong pie."

"They'd suit me fine, too," said Thrasher. Leave it to Baylor to think of food at a time like this.

Tim sat up. "I've been thinking about those baseball Yankees we met in Port Republic. They didn't seem all that different from us, did they?"

Thrasher could hear Baylor scratching himself. "They talked kind of funny, but they didn't look all that different," Baylor said. "But they got to be, or we wouldn't be fighting them."

Thrasher agreed. He had expected soulless eyes and horns growing out of the Yankees' foreheads. Instead, the baseball Yankees had seemed as tired and hungry and homesick as the Rebels.

He thought about the dead Yankees and Rebels buried back in Port Republic. When you were filling graves, the only difference between them was the color of their shirts beneath the blood and Virginia dust.

It hit Thrasher, all of a sudden, that all the bodies buried there—Yankee and Rebel alike—would eventually turn into the same rich Virginia soil. Death would make no distinction between the enemies at all.

For several minutes, Baylor, Tim, and Thrasher lay there, on their bedrolls, not saying a word.

"This here war makes me wonder," said Baylor finally. "Will I be lying on this raggedy old blanket tomorrow night, or will it be covering some other Reb?"

There was an awkward silence, like a question hanging in the air. Baylor cleared his throat. "I also been thinking on something else, too, Thrasher. I know I ain't been the best soldier. Not like you."

Like me? thought Thrasher, surprised.

"I made sport when I should've been doing my duty," said Baylor. "I know y'all felt hard toward me, and I can't say I blame you." He took a breath. "But Thrasher, you and me go way back, and we need a pact of some sort."

"What sort of pact?"

"Swear you'll look for me if I'm missing?"

Baylor's request startled Thrasher. "'Course I would. Don't you know that?"

"And if I'm a gone raccoon," said Baylor, "would you write my momma and tell her? Tell her I died the most glorious death—even if you got to make some of it up. It would mean a lot to her."

"Of course," said Thrasher. His voice cracked. Lord, it hurt to think about Baylor wounded—or even worse.

There was more silence, then Tim's voice came out of the darkness, sounding thin and jagged. "I always thought I'd have a lifetime to make things right with my family. But now I'm thinking that my lifetime may not be all that long."

But it could be. You don't have to be a soldier, Thrasher wanted to say. Instead, he whispered, "You don't have to fight."

"Oh, yes I do," she finally said. "Who you are is what you do—what you make of yourself." Her voice shook. "I've written a letter to my family. Tell me, Thrasher, if the worst comes for me, would you see that they get it?"

Thrasher rolled over, studied Tim's slender form, sitting in the darkness. He thought again on all that Tim had done—the marching, foraging, drilling, burying, and now tomorrow, fighting. Tim had declared herself, in all she had done. It dawned on Thrasher, slowly, that *what* Tim did was more important than *who* Thrasher thought she was.

"I'll make sure your family knows what a fine soldier you been," he said. "That you trailed them clouds of glory."

"How about you, Thrasher?" asked Baylor. "I can't write, but Tim can. What'll we tell your folks?"

Thrasher thought on it. "Tell my sisters I love them, even if they are pesty. Tell M'am I didn't take the Lord's name in vain, and I didn't chew tobacco or drink liquor except for that one time you tricked me into sipping that watermelon." He felt a shudder of self-pity as he imagined himself lying dead, never having done any of those things.

"What about your pap?" asked Baylor.

Thrasher paused. What could he tell Pap? "Tell him I settled a score."

CHAPTER

16

THE NEXT MORNING, Baylor's blanket was bare, and Thrasher wondered where he had gone. A sudden thought struck him: Maybe Baylor had run off in the night.

He got up, stretched, looked around. No Baylor. Around the camp, men were creeping about, silent as ghosts, stooping to roll up blankets, sitting to finish a letter or read their testaments or pray, lifting a final cup of coffee, or eating hotcakes and biscuits.

Wade seemed in better humor as he stood in line near the supply wagon, waiting for his quota of cartridges. He was joking with another man. Five other men were counting their rounds of ammunition. Several more were checking and rechecking their guns.

They wiped the steel of their bayonets until they shone.

Still, there was no Baylor, and Thrasher found himself growing concerned.

Goodloe was washing up in a trough of muddy water, and Tim waited behind him. "Y'all see Baylor?" asked Thrasher.

Goodloe shook his head and splashed his face again.

"I heard him get up last night," said Tim. "He didn't say where he was going."

Hazen emerged from behind the supply wagon. His mustache looked freshly waxed. He was wearing his red battle shirt and sported tall black boots and a floppy black hat. One side of the hat was pinned up and decorated with a feather.

Wade catcalled from the supply wagon, "Come up out of them boots, Hazen. We know you're in there. We can see your arms sticking out."

Hazen scowled but said nothing. He fastened his cartridge belt around his waist.

Thrasher washed up after Goodloe and Tim. The water smelled dank, and he wondered how many others had used it that morning. He wiped his face on his shirt.

He looked up to see Baylor straggling toward him.

Baylor's eyes were bloodshot, and his face was puffy from lack of sleep.

"There you are," said Thrasher, relieved.

"'Course I'm here. Where else would I be?"

Thrasher didn't say. He felt a little foolish about it.

"Been visiting some of the boys from other companies," Baylor told him. "Didn't you hear? We're forming the last line, the tail of the march."

Hazen joined them in time to hear Baylor's news. "The tail!" said Hazen. "By the time we get there, won't be anything to do except clean up."

"Who's up front?" asked Goodloe. He wiped his glasses for the hundredth time.

"Jackson's Stonewall Brigade," answered Baylor. He was clearly proud to have something important to report. "You should've seen them whooping it up. They're pop-eyed as bullfrogs with the excitement of it all."

Thrasher wanted to find out more, but the regimental drums rolled. Company after company hurried into formation. They fell into place, lined up shoulder to shoulder. Thrasher stood between Baylor and Tim.

Major Wilmot approached on a mud-splattered gray gelding. The men grinned at him and gave him sloppy salutes. The major returned the salutes.

"In a few minutes," the major shouted, "we'll be moving out. We have a long march ahead of us. Save your water for battle. You'll receive final instructions on the field."

The snare drum rolled, and a bugle flared. Thrasher's heart beat rapidly.

"Forward, march!" shouted Wilmot.

THOUSANDS OF FEET tramped. Thousands of tin cups clinked against thousands of cartridge belts. Ahead, the long columns of men wound as far as Thrasher could see. Their shouldered guns spiked the air. Everywhere he looked, he saw gray: gray morning mist, gray dust, gray men.

The sun poked through the treetops. Morning grew alive with birdcalls, the flutter of wings, and the hum of cicadas. The regiment marched past homes, barns, fences without rails, fields without corn, and cows resting in the shade of trees. Womenfolk met them along the way and offered pails of fresh water.

Some of the men took off their hats and bowed in a grand gesture to the women. "Good morning to y'all," they called out, as if they were strolling to Sunday church.

Others shouted apologies as they tramped through

fields and orchards. "Sorry about the mess we're making."

"Tell me your name," said Baylor to girl after girl. "I'll name my musket after you." He promised to look up each new sweetheart when the war ended.

"Before today's over," said Thrasher, "you'll be promised to a dozen girls."

"Ain't war grand?" said Baylor.

Tim rolled her eyes.

They passed forests of pine, ash, and poplar. From one broad-leafed maple, a yellow bird flitted from branch to branch. "Sweet-sweet-sweet," it chirruped.

"This ain't so sweet," said Thrasher, mopping his forehead with his sleeve.

Soon the sun burned to a yellow blaze above the trees, and birdcalls stopped, as if every winged creature had flown away. Thrasher scratched beneath his damp jacket.

Still, they marched. He could barely feel his feet and legs. He narrowed his eyes to keep out the dust and concentrated on the heels of the man ahead of him. Marching was easiest if he didn't look to see how far it was to the top of the next hill or how patiently the buzzards stared down from their treetops.

The sun slipped to the other side of noon. Soft dust

billowed over Thrasher, and his mouth turned dry as cotton. His teeth felt gritty from the dirt. He unplugged his canteen and lifted it to his lips.

A hand gripped his arm. "Not too much," warned a gray-haired man. "You'll need it later."

It didn't make sense to Thrasher. Why save water for battle when he needed it now? But the man's voice was so formidable that Thrasher listened. In his mind, he imagined up an endless supply of cool swamp water, drawn from the depths of a gator hole.

BY LATE AFTERNOON, they heard the first boom of artillery and the crackle of musketry. At first, it sounded like bacon frying in a large skillet. Then it sounded like a canebrake fire that turned into a terrific thunderstorm.

Soon the regiment diverged from the main road, and Thrasher found himself up to his knees in mud. He slogged through the swampy ground. With each artillery boom, the earth quivered, and the air curdled with sulfur and dirt.

Major Wilmot approached on his horse. "Yankees," he shouted, "lie along a ridge in the wilderness between us and the Chickahominy River. General Ewell is being sorely pressed. He needs reinforcements!"

"That's us," Thrasher said to Tim.

Major Wilmot heard and nodded. "Your job is to drive the Yankees out and take the ridge."

The men let out high yips of Rebel joy. They ran to drop their haversacks beneath a large oak tree.

The order was shouted to form the line. Thrasher took his place between Tim and Baylor and sucked in a long breath. This was it, the moment he had been waiting for since he'd walked out of the swamp two months ago.

He looked at the faces of those around him. Some moved their lips in prayer, and some studied testaments.

He tried to remember bits of prayer—something about lying down in green pastures and a rod and a staff to comfort him—but he couldn't, so he made up his own: *Lord, help me be brave.*

Wilmot and his horse stood in front of the men, ready to address them. His eyes shone as he spoke. "Soon we will engage the enemy. Remember my instructions: Do not shoot until you're within effective musket range. Single out *one* adversary for your fire. Whenever possible, pick off the enemy's officers, particularly the mounted ones, and the artillery horses."

Wilmot paused. He seemed to take in the gaze of

each man. "Do not heed the calls of wounded comrades or stop to take them to the rear."

Those were the most difficult orders of all. Thrasher looked at Goodloe wiping his glasses again. Baylor was swallowing hard, and Tim shifted uncomfortably from foot to foot. How could Thrasher not stop to help them?

"Provisions have been made for the wounded," said Wilmot. "The best way to protect your friends is to drive the enemy from the field. Do your duty in a manner that honors the heroic example your comrades have set on earlier fields of combat."

"Cowards will be shot!" shouted Hazen, his fist punching the air.

Wilmot fixed a steely gaze on Hazen. "As for you, consider ridding yourself of that red shirt—unless you want to be the center target of every enemy gun."

Hazen withered. He fell out of line and ran back to the oak tree, where he tore off his shirt and dug through his bedroll for another one.

Baylor nudged Thrasher. "Aw. What'd he go and tell him that for?"

Wilmot raised his saber in the air. "Huzzah for old Georgia forever!"

"Huzzah!" yelled the Rebel troops.

A grapeshot canister arced over the ridge and

whistled toward them. It exploded, spitting bits of metal and littering the air with white flakes. Thrasher cringed at the men's screams and the sight of the bright red blood on their faces and arms. Wilmot's horse reared and pawed the air.

The Rebel artillery retaliated, clouding the air with gray smoke.

"Charge!" screamed Wilmot, flashing his saber.

A Rebel yell burst forth from the men. Coattails swirled, and Thrasher was swept along as they sprang forward.

17

THE FIRST ONE HUNDRED yards felt like walking into the wind. A storm of minie balls whistled past as Thrasher advanced slowly with his company. They formed a straight line, and the sun glinted off their guns.

With shaky legs, he passed clumps of splintered trees and waded knee-deep through a stream. He told himself he would not run.

In front of him lay a rocky field. Beyond that was the top of the hill. And beyond that, he knew, were the Yankees.

With each rain of bullets, screams of joy and pain and rage filled the air. Men from his company appeared through the smoke, then disappeared, like deer leaping through woods. He saw Tim kneel and ram powder into her gun. He saw Goodloe one second and nodded at him. The next second, Goodloe's eyes rolled back until only the whites showed, and he sprawled forward.

Horrified, Thrasher moved on. He tried not to think of Goodloe. More men fell around him in a spray of blood and flesh. His hands weren't his hands now, carrying the gun. His feet weren't his feet, stepping over maimed bodies.

A handsome young officer rode up on a chestnut horse. Thrasher looked again, and the horse was riderless as it galloped past. Its eyes were wild, and blood streamed from its muzzle.

A yellow-haired boy in front of Thrasher exploded to bits, splattering Thrasher's face and uniform with blood and gore. He wiped at it, saw it wasn't his own, and advanced.

Men lay tangled on the ground, groaning and clawing. Thrasher and the line of Georgians advanced over them. Sometimes they walked, sometimes they crawled like turkey hunters through brush. Where an opening formed in the line, other men dropped in and closed it up. Thrasher couldn't help but think how simply it was done, like filling the chinks between logs.

The man next to him screamed and lurched forward, his chest ripped wide open.

Another man swore violently and clutched his stomach. His innards spilled out between his hands.

Still, Thrasher moved forward, always forward. His eyes burned from the smoke, but he continued on. He thrust the rod into his gun, singled out an adversary, then fired.

To his right, he saw a man crawling. The man still fired, even though his chin had been blown away. Thrasher recognized another boy, a birdlike boy with a skinny neck. He was kneeling, tying a dirty cloth around his bleeding leg. A burly man cursed as he limped forward, dragging his bloody foot.

The smoke turned yellow. He saw colorful flags, shells bursting in air, white flakes floating, and trees. Then, for the first time, he saw the line of bluecoats. They were firing from behind the trees.

Instinctively, he dropped to the ground. The earth shook beneath him. He tore at the grass and the dirt, swearing and cursing the Yankees. The flames and smoke bit at him.

Cover, he thought. *I need cover.* A few hundred feet away, he saw a mound of rocks. He concentrated on them.

He stuffed cartridge after cartridge into his gun, firing all the while as he half-crawled, half-dashed through brambles, dirt, and over bodies toward the rocks. Each time he pulled the trigger, he grunted as if he were pounding each Yankee with his own fist.

The wind shifted. His ears filled with the roar of shells. The yellow smoke enveloped him, burning his eyes, catching in his throat. Then the smoke turned white. Colorful battle flags floated like red and yellow birds. More shells burst, and then, just as suddenly, the guns died down. An eerie stillness hung over the air.

The charge was over, and, miraculously, he had reached the rocks. He crouched by them and rubbed his cheek against them. He reveled in their rough, hard feel. *I done it,* he wanted to shout. *I'm alive!*

He looked at his feet, his legs, his arms, and his hands, and he was Thrasher again. He had done what he'd had to do, what Jackson had asked him to do. *This is how it feels to be a man.* He would never doubt himself again.

Feeling exhilarated, he crept to the side of the rocks to look for his company—for Baylor, for Tim, for Goodloe. For anyone he knew.

THE FIELD WAS studded with bloodied bodies. Everywhere he saw writhing arms and legs. Everywhere he heard weeping and groaning.

The shakes started. First his knees, then his arms and hands. *O Lord, what did we do?*

He licked his cracked lips and propped his musket against a rock. His fingers and hands continued to shake as he struggled with the stopper to his canteen. He pulled the stopper and held the canteen to his lips.

Empty.

In disbelief, he turned the canteen over and saw the bullet hole. He fingered the ragged edges of the hole. His knees buckled. How close the bullet had come to him! Nervously, he licked his cracked lips again. His tongue felt too swollen for his mouth. He looked for water.

A short distance away, he saw three riderless horses near a stream. He picked up his gun and started toward the water. His legs wobbled as he stepped around bloody bodies, dressed in blue and in gray.

Just as he reached the water's edge, a grizzly-bearded Yankee rose up on his knees from the other side, swaying, a gun in his hands.

In a flash, Thrasher trained his gun on the Yankee. But then he saw the Yankee's eyes, dull with pain. The man was wounded. A belly wound. Blood was spreading, roselike, over his uniform.

"Go ahead," the man said. "Shoot me."

This Yankee seemed different from the ones in the woods. He hadn't seen their eyes, only the blue color of their uniforms. He lowered his gun.

The Yankee's eyes turned hard and gleaming. "You're soft, boy."

The words were sharp and cut deep inside Thrasher. He raised his gun. Suddenly, there was a roar that sounded like laughter. A gust of wind flapped Thrasher's shirt, grabbed his canteen, and flung it aside. It picked Thrasher up, then dropped him, shoving his face into the dirt.

He touched the ground beneath him. With surprise, he saw that his fingers were wet with blood. His blood.

Ain't no pain, he thought.

I expected pain.

Don't I deserve pain?

CHAPTER

18

THRASHER'S EYES fluttered, but they were heavy, and it hurt too much to open them. The pain up his left arm and through his shoulder came in waves. Only the darkness seemed to subdue it.

He had dreamed of tea-colored water, bearded trees, a punt boat, and Chum. But now he thought of Baylor and their pact, and he wondered if Baylor would come. He listened to the gentle ripple of water, and a little above that, a droning sound, like a hive of bees. The drone thickened, and with it, the smell thickened, too—the greasy, coiled smell that comes with death. Just like Port Republic.

He drifted off again. Night came, then morning, and then, finally, a faraway voice: "Thrasher, is that you?"

Thrasher moaned. Everything hurt, but his chest and arm hurt most of all. With each breath, fresh pain stabbed him. Was he dying? Living was too painful. "Lemme be," he said hoarsely.

The voice was closer now, somewhere above him. "And let my best friend in the whole world die?"

Thrasher barely opened his eyes. The morning sun scratched at them. He saw a bloody cloth wrapped around Baylor's head.

"If you . . . don' . . . lemme . . . die," Thrasher said, "I'll . . . haunt you . . . when I do."

Baylor persisted. "I ain't about to figure out what to say in no letter for you. That was only the deal if you was dead already."

Thrasher shut his eyes again. *O Lord.* Sometimes Baylor just wore him out.

Baylor knelt by Thrasher. "Looky here."

Thrasher squinted. A tawny head with a black nose and bright eyes poked out of Baylor's jacket. The pup licked Baylor's face.

"I found this Yankee pup all curled up on his poor master's chest," Baylor said. "Crying like nobody's business. 'Course I'd cry, too, if I was a Yankee."

"You . . . stole . . . some . . . dead . . . Yank's . . . dog?" Thrasher moaned. *Glory, it hurts to talk.*

"He's a Rebel dog now," said Baylor, sounding hurt. "Even a dog's got the right to be raised up proper. And I didn't steal him. I adopted him. His name's Bugle."

"Sor—ry," said Thrasher. Baylor could make his head spin. He closed his eyes again.

"You're forgiven. Now stay awake, and listen up. Don't you go shutting your eyes. Look at all I foraged."

Thrasher cracked his eyes open again. Baylor set the pup on the stream bank. From his dirt-covered jacket, he took out three biscuits, a gold pocketwatch, and a cased photograph of a girl in a white lace dress.

"This girl don't have no name, so I named her Meredith after my musket." He swung the pocketwatch on its chain. "Where that Yankee is, time don't matter now."

Thrasher groaned.

"Now was that an 'I hurt' groan, or one of your 'I-don't-believe-you-did-that' groans?"

Thrasher felt Baylor studying him. "I can tell what you're thinking," said Baylor. "But I waited for that Yank to die. Even shared my canteen with him. Now to others, it might not make much difference, but to me, it don't feel right emptying a feller's pockets while he's still got a few breaths left in him—even if he is a Yankee."

"You're . . . an . . . honor—'ble . . . man," said Thrasher. He licked his cracked lips and tasted blood. A new stab of pain raced up his arm. He felt a swooning darkness, but he refused to give in to it. He had to know about the others.

"Where's Tim?"

Baylor hesitated. "Litter bearers took him off." His voice sounded torn at the edges. "He's messed up pretty bad. Hazen's all right. Ain't seen Goodloe yet."

A picture of Goodloe passed in and out of Thrasher's mind. He tried to hold it there long enough to remember, but it hurt too much.

"Wade's been shot through the hand," said Baylor. "Blew his thumb right off." He lowered his voice. "Some are saying Wade shot himself on purpose. He was blubbering about his sons and wanting to get home to them."

Wade? So strong. So sure of himself. Thrasher could imagine Hazen shooting his own thumb off, maybe, but not Wade.

Baylor cleared his throat. "Listen, Thrasher, ol' buddy, I'm going to pull you out of here and get you some help."

"I . . . can't," said Thrasher.

"You can," said Baylor firmly. "You was man enough to get yourself shot. I reckon that makes you man enough to stand just about anything. Now turn your head. This is going to hurt, and I don't want to see your face when it does."

Baylor lifted him, and fire licked through Thrasher, up his left arm and down to his rib cage. "Your arm looks like it's been chomped on by a gator," said Baylor. "And from the looks of you, you lost a lot of blood. But don't you think about that just now. Consider yourself lucky it ain't no belly wound."

Baylor carried Thrasher over the hill, crisscrossing between craters and piles of dead. Everywhere, moaning, groaning, and weeping hung in the air like a heavy storm cloud.

A merciful blackness fell upon Thrasher again.

THRASHER HAD NO idea how long it had taken them to get to the hospital. He had a vague memory of clinging to Baylor across fields, then stumbling alongside him down a long dirt road. They joined a stream of wounded soldiers. The last part of the journey, they rode in a wagon that almost jarred his teeth loose.

Suddenly he remembered the daisies, too, clumps and clumps of them in bloom along the road. They stood at attention like proud soldiers. He thought of M'am and the fistfuls of daisies he used to bring to her. She always set the daisies in a jar of water on the table.

Now, as he lay in the grass on the hospital grounds, the faraway rumblings of artillery set the earth to trembling again. It sounded like the distant boom of the swamp. He wished he were there now, in his cabin, or better yet, poling across the prairie waters, with Chum sitting in the bow of his punt. *How much longer will the fighting last?* he wondered. *Where are the Yankees now?*

He blinked. His left arm didn't hurt now. It just lay there, white and swollen and caked with dried blood. Nearby, Baylor was crouched next to someone.

"Baylor?" Thrasher called softly.

"Me and Tim are right here."

Thrasher lifted his head and saw Tim's soft brown hair. "Tim?" he called softly.

No answer.

"Tim," he called again, as loud as he could muster.

"She's still with us," said Baylor. He coughed to clear his throat, but his voice still wavered as he spoke. "She wants us to send her belongings to her family."

She wants. Her belongings. So Baylor knows.

"Tell Tim . . . to get better—" Thrasher gasped for a breath. "And take care of her own belongings."

Baylor bent over Tim. "That's our first plan, ain't it, Tim?"

Thrasher closed his eyes. He tried to think about Tim, but his thoughts grew hazy. A pleasant picture of all of them playing baseball at Camp Semmes drifted into his mind—Wade's swing tearing the yarn from the ball, Goodloe pitching, Tim running home, Baylor hollering everybody on. It was so long ago. The picture faded away.

Thrasher cracked open his eyes and saw Bugle lying near Baylor. The pup's head rested on his front paws, and his sorrowful brown eyes watched everything, just like Chum. The pup's ears twitched with the booms of the distant cannon.

Thrasher wiggled the fingers on his good hand and coaxed Bugle over. He wanted to feel the loose folds of the pup's neck. Bugle obliged and licked Thrasher's hand.

He closed his eyes again and imagined it was Chum.

"Thrasher—" said Baylor.

"Yeah?"

"Some boys wrote themselves furlough passes to go home."

"You?"

"Naw. Not me. I figure it's about time I did some of that duty you're always harping on. I thought you might like to know that." Baylor cleared his throat and changed the subject. "You hear we won at Gaines' Mill?"

So the battle had a name. Thrasher hadn't thought to ask.

"We pushed them Yankees clear across the Chickahominy. Us Rebs slept on the battlefield that night. General Lawton said we earned the right to sleep on the ground we fought so hard to win. 'Course I couldn't sleep 'cause I was too busy looking for you."

Thrasher smiled. Baylor's voice grew fuzzy and far-away. "The way we all fought, this war'll be over real soon." Then Thrasher fell to sleep again.

WHEN HE WOKE, the sun was climbing. It was noticeably hotter, and the smell was growing. For the first time, he noticed hundreds of wounded men, lying like him, in the sun.

He squinted. A short distance away, he saw a dozen men digging graves. Some were using spades; others scooped the earth with tin cups and plates. The dead were being placed in rows.

Slowly, Thrasher turned his head. Next to the surgeon's tent was a wagon filled with severed arms and legs, some still dressed in shirtsleeves or stockings and boots. He looked at his own swollen hand. *O Lord,* he prayed. *Please don't take mine.*

Baylor sat cross-legged between Thrasher and Tim.

"You're awake," he said to Thrasher. "Did I tell you I saw Jackson?"

"You did?" Thrasher tried to lift his head, but pain pushed it back down.

"He was sitting on his horse, holding his hand in the air, like he was testing which way the war was blowing. Seemed a crazy thing to do. Suppose somebody shot it?"

"Jackson ain't crazy."

"Some folks are saying Jackson didn't get us here fast enough. Some say he waited too long."

"We moved as fast as we could," said Thrasher. It hurt to do this much thinking. "All that rain and mud."

"I know," said Baylor. "Still, I can't help but wonder, maybe, just maybe, those folks is right. Maybe Jackson could've done more."

"No," said Thrasher. *They ain't right. Can't people see that? How could any of us have done more?*

He wanted to hear more, to say more, but two men came and bent over Tim. One of the men shook his head hopelessly. "No use," he said to the other. "This one's too far gone." The litter bearers moved on to another soldier.

Too far gone! Thrasher struggled to sit up, to call the men back. "Baylor," he cried. "Tell them. Tell them they're wrong."

Baylor's eyes filled with tears. Thrasher had never seen Baylor so serious, so worn out, so used up, and it frightened him. "They ain't wrong, Thrasher," Baylor whispered. "Tim's tore up mighty bad. A belly wound. Lost an awful lot of blood. I reckon all we can do is wait."

Baylor squatted closer to Tim. "We're here," he said in a gentle voice. "Just think on all them green pastures and still waters and trailing clouds of glory."

THE WAIT WASN'T LONG. Tim's chest heaved twice, then her throat rattled terribly. Baylor leaned over and pressed his cheek against Tim's. Then he sat on his knees, not saying a word, his back to Thrasher. His shoulders were hunkered down, and his hands were dug into his pockets, as if he didn't know what to do with them.

Thrasher felt chewed up with pain. He squeezed his eyes tight.

Suddenly, he sensed a shadow over him. He opened his eyes. The two litter bearers were standing over him, bending to pick him up.

"Baylor!" cried Thrasher as they lifted him up.

Baylor jumped up. He put his hand on the stretcher. "I'm right here. I'm coming."

The litter bearers carried Thrasher through the canvas opening of the surgeon's tent. They laid him on a blood-smeared table surrounded by four men in soiled aprons. The tent had the sickening-sweet smell of death.

He raised his head and looked wildly for Baylor. He spotted him standing in the tent opening. Thrasher swung his legs over the table's sides. "Baylor!" he cried. "Tell them my arm's all right. Don't let them take my arm!"

The men pushed Thrasher down onto the table. Gently, they pinned him there. Thrasher could see Baylor struggling for words. "Risk you ten dollars they don't," said Baylor.

The surgeon's face bobbed in front of Thrasher. Thrasher willed the fingers on his left hand to move, so the surgeon could see they weren't useless, but the fingers lay there, curled and white and swollen. Another man's face came forward, and a hand pressed a sweet-smelling rag against Thrasher's mouth.

Thrasher gasped for air, and then it was dark.

CHAPTER

19

SOMEWHERE, THE SWEETEST lullabies were being sung.

Thrasher looked down on the body that was his, lying on the table in the surgeon's tent.

He saw blood.

He saw the skin on his shoulder and arm laid open, so clean and white like pork.

Then he was inside the body that was his and he was thirsty, so thirsty.

His thoughts drifted by like clouds.

He saw himself, standing up to his knees in muck, at the edge of a black pool surrounded by blue pickerel-weed. Grasping his pole, he smacked his lips, the call to bring up a gator.

Nothing.

Disappointed, he jabbed his pole into the hole—once, twice.

Still nothing.

He stuck the pole between his teeth and smacked some more. His hands tingled as the sound traveled down the pole and into the murky water.

The gator floated to the surface, with barely a ripple. Its filmy lids transformed into hard, black, discerning eyes that gleamed at him.

The gator taunted him. "You ain't never going to be a man," it said. "You're soft. A man never lets something take away what's his."

Its tail lashed, churning the water to tea-colored foam. Its jaws snapped and it bellowed. Then the gator thrashed some more, practically leaping from the water.

Thrasher pulled his knife from its sheath. He raised it above his head. He readied himself for the dull *thwack!* of the knife through the gator's spine.

"I'm Thrasher Magee," he said. "I do what *I* want." Slowly, deliberately, he lowered the knife and put it away.

CHAPTER

20

THRASHER WAS THIRSTY. He strayed from the winding pathway that led to his cabin and walked to the water's edge. He set his haversack down and squatted. He dipped his fingers in the water. It felt warm. Cupping his hand, he made a small whirlpool and scooped some up to drink. It was refreshing.

When this war is over, I'd be grateful if you'd take me poling.

He opened his haversack and poked through Tim's belongings—a few articles of clothing, her pearl-handled knife, the letter she had written to her family, and her photograph.

He had thought about reading Tim's letter, all those weeks in the army hospital. But he couldn't bring himself to do it. He took out Tim's photograph and stared at her picture. "I made you a promise," he said. "And I intend to keep it."

Here, the war seemed so far away. He thought of Baylor, and wondered where he was now. Thrasher had offered to take Bugle home, but Baylor refused, saying, "A feller's got to have somebody. Don't you worry none. I'll learn Bugle to sit at attention and snap off a salute."

Thrasher stood, slung his haversack over his shoulder, and began walking again. The whole swamp was breathing, whispering, singing with the sounds of late summer. It reminded him of the camp hospital, when he'd asked the doctor about the sweet lullabies he had heard while he was lying on the surgeon's table.

"Singing?" asked the doctor. *"There was no singing, son. You must have been hallucinating."*

It was some time before Thrasher figured out that the lullabies must have been the sound of the surgeon's saw. He looked at the stump that hung where his left elbow used to be. He wondered if he'd ever grow used to the phantom itches and pains.

The craziest notion struck him, making him laugh out loud: "Why, Baylor owes me ten dollars."

FURTHER UP, HIS CABIN came into sight. He stood by the hollow tree, taking it all in: the thick walls, M'am's yellow curtains, the hens flocking about, the hog grunting in its pen. He heard the girls fussing in the cabin and the soft, higher sound of M'am's voice.

He looked for Chum but didn't see him. He whistled. There was silence, then Chum's loud bay broke the evening air.

Ears flapping, he tore from the cabin, down the steps in one bound, across the yard, clear to where Thrasher stood waiting. Chum leaped at Thrasher, grabbing his hand in his mouth, licking it, biting it, whining, and wagging his whole body.

"You remember," said Thrasher, bending down. His heart felt full. Chum licked him from chin to ear, then flopped himself down and rolled over, begging for a belly scratch.

Thrasher obliged. "I hope you ain't grown into no lazy under-the-porch sleeper while I was gone."

"Lord, O Lord."

Thrasher looked up to see M'am standing on the porch. Her hand flew up to cover her mouth. Then she sat down on the rocker and cried into her apron.

He took long steps, heading for the porch quickly now. Chum followed at his heels. His sisters crowded themselves in the cabin doorway and peered at him. Thrasher could tell they didn't know what to make of him.

Mabel was first. She pushed past the two little ones and flew down the steps, arms spread wide. She grabbed Thrasher, pulled him to her, hugged him tight, and stepped back. She took him in all at once, from head to toe. Her gaze lingered on the empty sleeve pinned to his chest, then flew back to his face. She was smiling, but Thrasher could see the sadness in her eyes.

Rosalie toddled down the steps, cautiously, one at a time. Thrasher smiled. She had grown so big. "Uppy?" he asked.

She nodded and lifted her arms. Thrasher dropped his haversack, wrapped his good arm around her, swung her up, and squeezed her tight. He carried her up the steps and plunked her down next to M'am.

M'am's face was shining. He knelt and laid his head in her lap. "The good Lord brung you home to us," she said, through her tears.

Thrasher suddenly realized how much lap M'am had. "The baby?"

"A girl," said Pap.

Thrasher tensed as he stood slowly and faced Pap. Pap was standing in the doorway, holding the baby.

Mabel reached and took the baby from Pap.

"It's been a long time, boy," said Pap. "We been waiting on you."

Thrasher looked steadily into Pap's eyes. "I ain't a boy no more."

Pap's mouth formed a thin line as his jaw worked and his eyes grew soft. "No, I suppose you're not."

Pap reached out, touched Thrasher's shoulder hesitantly, then gripping more firmly, he drew him close the way he would Mabel or Rebecca or Rosalie. Thrasher felt no shame in the comfort of Pap's arms.

THRASHER WAS AWAKE early. He yanked his homespun shirt over his head and tucked it into the waist of his pants.

He went over to the kitchen table. He picked up a chunk of last night's corn bread, wrapped it inside his kerchief, and stuck it in the haversack. In the dim light, he could see Mabel, Rebecca, and Rosalie still sleeping. From the lean-to room, he heard Pap snort and toss. If anybody else was awake, no one let on. Thrasher was glad to have the morning to himself.

He tiptoed out of the cabin, where Chum was waiting for him, his tail wagging.

"Come on, boy," said Thrasher.

Nose to the ground, the dog trotted alongside Thrasher, down the path through the woods, to the water's edge.

The punt lay on the bank, bottom-side up. Thrasher picked it up and righted it. Chum jumped in, taking his place in the bow.

Thrasher tossed the haversack into the punt, then slid the boat into the water. It barely rocked as he climbed in. With his forked pole, he pushed off against the swamp bottom.

FROM THE CYPRESS LIMBS, moss wavered like old gray ghosts. Thrasher imagined the ghosts were guarding the swamp against Yankee intruders, even though he knew there weren't any Yankees around these parts. Most of the fighting was still taking place in Virginia.

Farther up, he broke out of the watery woods. On the prairie head now, he set the pole down and picked up the paddle. It was tricky work but not impossible.

Out in the open water, he saw a banded water snake curve gracefully past the boat, then disappear into the tall grass. The grass swayed gently against the breeze. He rested the paddle across the boat's rim. He reached for the haversack, opened it, took out Tim's photograph and the letter she had written to her family.

All through the jarring train ride back to Georgia,

crowded with hundreds of maimed soldiers, he had thought about this moment—his punt, Chum standing in the bow, the slow-moving waterways of the Okefinokee. This was where he would read Tim's letter. No other place would do.

CHAPTER

21

Dear Mama and Papa,

If you are reading these lines, it means the worst has come for me. Please forgive me if I have brought shame upon you. I simply could not be who you wanted me to be. I do not dream of marriage and china patterns the way some women do.

All my life, I could never imagine anything marvelous happening to me. How unfair it seemed that boys could dream to grow into the tallest oaks, but girls were destined to be the vine that clings to the oak.

Ever since I was a little girl, I have kept up with the boys. Remember how I sneaked away to play ball in the park until it was dark? Remember how angry the boys were because I was the swiftest runner? Remember,

Father, how angry you were when you found out about my ball playing? After that, you relegated my adventures to books that you chose for me, and Mother relegated my adventures to sewing circles and needlepoint.

When the war broke out, it was more than I could bear. Each day I read the newspapers and heard the stories of battles and skirmishes. Yet the only way I could serve my country was to collect lint, sew red-flannel cartridge bags, and knit woolen socks. I found myself envious of each Southern soldier. Army life was a thousand times more interesting than mine.

When it became clear that New Orleans might fall to the Yankees, I wanted to don pants and trounce those Yankees myself. Why shouldn't a woman be permitted to defend the honor of the country and people she loves?

Dear Mama and Papa, please do not cry for me. I hope you find solace in knowing that this is the life I chose.

> *Your loving daughter,*
> *Timothea*

THE BOAT DRIFTED AIMLESSLY along the Big Water.

Thrasher folded Tim's letter and placed it back in the haversack. He took out another sheet of paper and a pencil and began to write.

Deer Mister and Miz LaFaye,

My pap allwayz sed you cood judje a man by the respekt he shewed his work. Same can be sed about yore dawter Tim. She wuz a fine soljer, full of dooty and respekt. I wuz proud to serv longsid her.

He stopped and looked at what he had written. His handwriting didn't creep like vines the way Tim's did, and he knew he didn't spell all the words right the way Goodloe would have. But he thought about Tim. *Just tell it your own way.*

And Thrasher intended to. He thought about the watermelon whiskey, poker games, and baseball, and he chuckled. "Someday I'm going to tell it all," he told Chum. "All the adventures and all the soldiering, right from the start."

ALTHOUGH THRASHER MAGEE and his companions are fictional characters, the Twenty-sixth Regiment Georgia Volunteer Infantry, its company of Okefinokee Rifles, and its participation in the Seven Days' Battles were real. Some of the historical action leading to the Seven Days' Battles has been condensed; some of the day-to-day events are products of research and imagination.

Today, *Okefinokee* is spelled *Okefenokee*, an official spelling decision made nearly a century ago by the United States Geographical Board. I have used the time-honored spelling, *Okefinokee*, a name derived from the Creek word *O-ke-fin-o-cau*. The Creek word means "Land of the Trembling Earth," an apt description of the swamp's watery woods and floating islands.

The Okefinokee Rifles organized in August 1861, seven months after Georgia seceded from the Union, and they were stationed at Camp Semmes, Brunswick, Georgia. In May 1862, they received orders to travel by rail to Richmond, Virginia. "On those open cars and in the cold rain," wrote a private, "many of the boys got sick. Some died from the exposure."

When General Robert E. Lee saw the Twenty-sixth Georgia regiment, he was so impressed that he wrote to the Confederate secretary of war and said that he wished the regiment were being assigned to him instead of to Jackson. Indeed, although many of the Georgians were still in their late teens, they were tough outdoorsmen, skilled in hunting. During one battle in the Shenandoah Valley campaign, for instance, when the Yankees struck, the Twelfth Georgia was ordered to pull back into a more defensible line. They refused. Instead, they stood up to take better aim at the Yankees charging up the hill. Their stance made them targets, and the Georgians suffered great losses. The next day, one Georgian explained: "We did not come all this way to Virginia to run before the Yankees."

On June 7, 1862, the Twenty-sixth Georgia was ordered to join Stonewall Jackson in Virginia's Shenandoah Valley. They arrived at Port Republic one day after General Jackson had fought the last battle of his famous Valley Campaign.

The disappointed Georgians were assigned to the gruesome task of burying the dead. "The sights and smells that assailed us were simply indescribable," wrote one soldier. "Corpses swollen to twice their original size, some of them actually burst asunder with the pressure of foul gases and vapours. . . . In a short time we all sickened."

After the bodies were buried, the Georgians then joined Jackson's regiment. The ever-secretive Jackson wouldn't disclose where they were headed. For days they crisscrossed Virginia in open railroad cars and slogged on foot through rain. They finally arrived outside Richmond on June 24.

The first of the Seven Days' Battles, the Battle of Beaver Dam Creek, was fought without Jackson's regiment on June 26, 1862. When the battle ended, the Union army was still in position, and Lee's army was dangerously divided. The Confederates lost three times as many men as the Union.

For unknown reasons—possibly fatigue, stress, weather, lack of supplies, unreliable maps, Union sharpshooters—Jackson waited until June 27 to engage his troops in combat. The Confederates routed the Yankees, but their victory at Gaines' Mill was costly: They lost over 8,000 men. A newspaper correspondent reported that General Lawton gave his Confederate soldiers the right to sleep on the battlefield they had fought so hard to win. "What a resting place was that!" wrote the correspondent. "The ground wet with the blood of the brave, and the air vocal with the groans of the wounded and dying. The stars looked down upon the weary sleepers . . . and told them of a haven of everlasting peace and repose for the soldier who falls in defense of home, wife, and children."

Thrasher's story ends here, when victory still seemed possible for the South. Lee hoped to destroy the Union army before it reached the James River, but after the Battle of Malvern Hill on July 1, the Union army was safe at its new supply base on the James River. Of all the Seven Days' Battles, Gaines' Mill was the only victory for the South.

On July 4, Rebel and Yankee pickets near Malvern Hill called a truce to pick blackberries together. "Our boys and the Yanks made a bargain not to fire at each other," a Southern private wrote, "and went out in the field, leaving one man on each post with the arms, and gathered berries together and talked over the fight, traded tobacco and coffee and exchanged newspapers as peacefully and kindly as if they had not been engaged for the last seven days in butchering each other." Such instances of fraternization are well-documented in history books, diaries, letters, and newspaper accounts. Rebels and Yankees bantered and sneaked across picket lines to drink and play cards.

Rebels and Yankees also shared a love for sports, and baseball was the most popular. The rules differed considerably from today's: High scores were common, and base runners were struck out when they were "soaked," or struck by the ball. A Confederate soldier described the roughness of the game: "Frank Ezell was ruled out because he could throw harder and straighter than any man in the company. He came very near to knocking the stuffing out of three or four of the boys, and the boys swore they would not play with him." I've never been able to prove that a baseball game between Rebels and Yankees actually occurred; I have never been able to disprove the possibility, either.

Instances of humanity are documented, too. After battles, Rebels and Yankees shared their canteens with wounded and dying enemies and often found themselves working shoulder to shoulder, burying their dead. When one Southern burial detail lacked suitable tools, they borrowed shovels from the Yankees. Some soldiers even risked their lives by returning wounded and dying enemies to the other side. When Rebel and Yankee met, invariably they did talk about the war. After a long conversation with a Union soldier, one Confederate soldier decided, "We could have settled the war in thirty minutes, had it been left to us."

The minimum age for enlistment on both sides was eighteen. Boys like Thrasher, eager to fight and unwilling to lie, wrote *18* on scrips of paper and tucked them into their shoes so that they could say "I'm standing over eighteen today."

For many soldiers, slavery wasn't the issue. In fact, although some Confederate officers brought their slaves to camp to take care of their personal needs, most of the Southern infantrymen were too poor to own slaves. Like Baylor, many of these boys were looking for adventure. As one Confederate recruit said, "I want to fight the Yankees—all fun and frolic." As the war wore on, the South eventually passed a bill that allowed Southern blacks to fight for the Confederacy.

Like Tim, an estimated four hundred or more women from both sides disguised themselves as men so that they could fight for the land and the people they loved—or so that they could be near their soldier husbands. One woman soldier, whose identity was discovered by an army doctor tending her wounds, later explained to a nurse, "I thought I'd like camp life, and I did."

U   S   E   F   U   L   S   O   U   R   C   E   S

The following sources have been useful in creating the characters, developing the background for the novel, and re-creating the involvement of the Twenty-sixth Georgia regiment in the days leading up to and including the Gaines' Mill Battle. Other useful sources include my husband, Joe, who teaches American history to seventh-grade students; friends and Georgians Mary Joyce and Goodloe Love; Civil War historian Dick Garrison; my writers group; and seventh-generation Okefinokee swamper Luther Thrift.

Botkin, B.A. *A Civil War Treasury of Tales, Legends, and Folklore*. New York: Random House, 1960.

Brocket, L.P., M.D. *Women at War: A Record of Their Patriotic Contributions, Heroism, Toils, and Sacrifice During the Civil War*. Stamford, Connecticut: Longmeadow Press, 1993.

The Civil War, 28 vols. Alexandria, Virginia: Time-Life Books, 1987.

Commager, Henry Steele, ed. *The Blue and the Gray: The Story of the Civil War as Told by Participants*. New York: Bobbs-Merrill Co., 1950.

Daily Crescent. New Orleans, Louisiana, 1862.

Daily Dispatch. Richmond, Virginia, 1862.

Davis, Burke. *They Called Him Stonewall: A Life of Lt. General T.J. Jackson, C.S.A.* 1954. Reprint. New York: Wings Books, 1988.

———. *Gray Fox: Robert E. Lee and the Civil War*. Reprint. New York: Fairfax Press, 1956.

Davis, William. *The Civil War Cookbook*. New York: Courage Books, 1993.

Dowdey, Clifford. *The Seven Days: The Emergence of Lee*. Lincoln, Nebraska: University of Nebraska Press, 1993.

Foote, Shelby. *The Civil War*. 3 vols. New York: Random House, 1958.

Harper, Francis and Delma E. Presley. *Okefinokee Album*. Athens, Georgia: Brown Thrasher Books, University of Georgia Press, 1981.

Harwell, Richard B., ed. *The Confederate Reader: How the South Saw the War*. New York: Dover Publications, 1989.

Langdon, William Chauncy. *Everyday Things in American Life, 1776–1876*. New York: Charles Scribner's Sons, 1941.

McPherson, James. *Ordeal by Fire*. New York: McGraw-Hill, Inc., 1982.

McQueen, A.S. and Hamp Mizell. *History of the Okefenokee Swamp*. Clinton, South Carolina: Jacobs and Co., 1954.

McWhiney, Grady. *Cracker Culture: Celtic Ways in the Old South*. Tuscalousa, Alabama: 1988.

Murfin, James V. *Battlefields of the Civil War*. Goldalming, England: Colour Library Books, 1988.

Murray, Alton. *South Georgia Rebels: The True Wartime Experiences of the 26th Regiment Georgia Volunteer Infantry, Lawton-Gordon-Evans Brigade*. St. Marys, Georgia: 1976.

National Geographic. *Realm of the Alligator*. Video. 1993.

Neill, Wilfred, T. *The Last of the Ruling Reptiles: Crocodiles, Alligators, and Their Kin*. New York: Columbia University Press, 1971.

Sanger, Marjorie Bartlett. *Cypress Country*. New York: World Publishing Co., 1965.

Savannah Republican. Savannah, Georgia, 1862.

Shep, R.L. *Civil War Era Etiquette: Martine's Handbook and Vulgarisms in Conversation*. 1866. Reprint. Mendocino, California: 1988.

Steinberg, Warren. *Masculinity: Identity Conflict and Transformation*. New York: Random House, 1993.

Walker, Laura Singleton. *History of Ware County, Georgia*. Macon, Georgia: J.W. Burke Co., 1934.

Ward, Geoffrey. *The Civil War: An Illustrated History*. New York: Alfred A. Knopf, Inc., 1990.

Wellikoff, Alan. *Civil War Supply Catalogue: A Comprehensive Sourcebook of Products from the Civil War Era Available Today*. New York: Crown Publishers, Inc., 1996.

Wiley, Bell Irvin. *The Life of Billy Yank: The Common Soldier of the Union*. Baton Rouge, Louisiana: Louisiana State University, 1984.

———. *The Life of Johnny Reb: The Common Soldier of the Confederacy*. Baton Rouge, Louisiana: Louisiana State University, 1984.

SUSAN CAMPBELL BARTOLETTI was inspired to write *No Man's Land* in 1992, after taking a course on the Civil War. She was fascinated by the acts of camaraderie that existed between the Rebels and the Yankees—examples of humanity not limited by the color of a man's uniform. Her studies compelled her to write about the teenage men who fought in the Civil War in search of adventure, and she was particularly drawn toward exploring the Southern point of view.

Ms. Bartoletti further researched the events for this novel by reading newspapers and histories from the Civil War era, studying old photographs, listening to contemporary nineteenth-century music, and trying recipes from Civil War cookbooks. She visited the Okefenokee Swamp, where she learned how to "call up" an alligator, and then spent several days talking with native "swampers" about their land and their relatives who had fought in the war. At the end of her trip, she visited numerous battlegrounds, following the route once traveled by the Twenty-sixth Georgia regiment.